THE BBC NATIONAL SHORT STORY AWARD 2017

The BBC National
Short Story Award
2017

in association with

First published in Great Britain in 2017 by Comma Press.
www.commapress.co.uk

A CIP catalogue record of this book is available
from the British Library.

ISBN 1910974358
ISBN-13 9781910974353

The publisher gratefully acknowledges the support
of Arts Council England.

Set in Bembo 11/13
Printed and bound in England by Clays

Contents

Introduction

I am a fervent admirer of the short story as a genre, and therefore thrilled to have witnessed its revival in the last decade, no small thanks to prizes such as this one, the BBC National Short Story Award with Booktrust. So, of course, I was more than delighted to be asked to chair this year's award and to help gather together such a rich and imaginative shortlist of new stories, all of which will be broadcast, as well as published within these pages. Hearing the stories read aloud on stage and on air is a real highlight of the award, especially given the ability of the short story to create intimacy between writer and reader.

My own view is that short stories are fiendishly difficult to get right. Narrative is clearly vital, but the sheer brevity of the genre – five or six thousand words, the length of a conventional novel's chapter – can be a particular challenge for some writers. In any case, the narrative of a short story has to be significant, almost metaphorical, so that the reader feels that this brief thing is a condensed version of something much bigger. At its best, a short story starts a process of thinking and imagining for a reader, a trigger, if you like, for all kinds of future thoughts and wonderings. I'm proud to say that this year's shortlist has achieved precisely that – characters, places and ideas that will linger with you long after you have finished reading.

Of course, I wasn't alone in the process of selecting the five finalists published here from the 600-plus entries submitted for the award. In fact, I saw my own role as much more that of listening and guiding than voicing an opinion, especially in the company of such a formidably qualified judging team, three of them award-winning writers themselves – Eimear McBride, Jon McGregor and Sunjeev Sahota – and a fourth, Di Speirs, who is not only the BBC's Books Editor, but is probably better read than any of us.

But as a process, it is as fair as it could possibly be made. The entries are all read by an experienced team of sifters, and then the resulting best 60 or so are handed to the judging panel without any indication – this is very important – of who wrote what. No names, no gender, no ethnicity, nothing but the stories themselves. At this point, any judge could call in any extra stories that they wanted to, and in our case, two judges called in a couple, two rather more, and one (me) none at all.

When it came to selecting the final five, I can truthfully say that no voices were raised. But some of the judges fought their corners for particular stories with a tenacity that would surely gladden the hearts of the authors. Inevitably, there has to be compromise, even disappointment, especially among judges with such disparate tastes – all valid! – and in a year when there were many excellently written stories and we could potentially have had a shortlist of ten rather than five. So there was vigourous debate and strenuous pleading and finally, a list. Our final five are, as you will see, very different, very compelling and very well written – original, accessible and finely crafted were the criteria that we had in mind throughout. They showcase a wide range of styles and subjects, and are all, interestingly and unusually, all by writers who have made their names as novelists as well as short story writers. This perhaps indicates the growth of the genre, but also how many more, and particularly younger writers, now see the short story as equally deserving of their time and effort.

These stories are printed in strictly alphabetical order so that nothing whatsoever can be read into the sequence. So I shall start with 'Murmur' by Will Eaves, who was Arts Editor of the Times Literary Supplement for almost 20 years. He is a published novelist and poet, and this story, set in the early 50's, is a quiet and horrifying account of a homosexual academic attempting to live his intellectual and sexual life while battling with enforced chemical castration. It is deliberately restrained in the writing, which only emphasises the dreadfulness of the narrative.

The second story is Jenny Fagan's 'The Waken'. Jenny is a shortlisted novelist for many prizes, on the Granta list of Best Young Novelists in 2013 (three out of our five were on this list), and writer in residence at Edinburgh University. 'The Waken' is a transfixing and powerful story about a Scottish girl on the Hebridean island of her childhood before her detested father's funeral, with all its myths and superstitions. As the ancient rites and rituals are performed Jessie undergoes a transformation, freeing her from her forbidding father. The reader becomes utterly absorbed in this visceral world of legend – no doubt precisely what the author intended.

Then comes Cynan Jones' 'The Edge of the Shoal'. Cynan Jones is a published novelist, an award winner – including the Wales Book of the Year Fiction Prize – and a widely translated writer of short stories. Ostensibly a story of man against nature, this is a lyrically, poetically written account, lit with poignancy, of a canoeist whose impulsive decision to change his plans leaves him struggling for survival. He has left a note for his partner – 'Pick salad' – but after catching the single fish he set out to, he finds himself wondering if he will ever see her again. Read on, for the consequences.

The fourth story is 'The Collector' by Ben

Markovits. Ben grew up on both sides of the Atlantic, has published seven novels, a trilogy on the life of Lord Byron, and is a frequent and acclaimed reviewer as well as a teacher of Creative Writing at Royal Holloway College. 'The Collector' is a beautifully written, atmospheric story of an eccentric loner on the Canadian border, who cannot stop filling his decaying house with things he intends to sell, but always replaces with yet more. And of his mysterious wife, who has departed as mysteriously as she arrived leaving him and the reader with many unanswered questions.

And finally, Helen Oyeyemi with 'If a book is locked there's probably a good reason for that, don't you think'. Helen has won the Somerset Maugham Award and the PEN Open Book Award for short stories, among other prizes. There is more mystery here, and a brilliant ending to the story of charismatic Eva, arriving to work in an office in an unknown city, and subtly creating mayhem with all manner of unexplained happenings and questions. And there's a locked diary which spills out of her handbag. Why is it locked? Why, indeed.

Joanna Trollope
London, 2017

Murmur

Will Eaves

FEAR OF HOMOSEXUALS IS never far from the surface. The few people who have supported me after my conviction must be very strong-minded. I do not think most people are equipped to associate with pariahs. They have a shadowy sense of how frail they themselves would be in the face of institutional opposition and stigmatisation, how utterly cast down they would be if they lost their jobs, if people they knew stopped serving them in shops or looked past them in the street. It is not hatred that turns the majority against the minority, but intuitive shame.

★

Do I need to set down the circumstances? The results are in the papers, and for once in my life I am disinclined to 'show my working'. It is strangely more instructive, for me, to imagine other conditions, other lives. But here they are, so that

1

my friends, when they come to these few thoughts, may do likewise.

I had just finished a paper and decided to award myself a pick-up. I met the boy, Cyril, on the fairground. He seemed undernourished and shifty but not unengaging; living, he said, in a hostel, working casually. I bought him pie and chips on the grounds and invited him home for the weekend. He didn't turn up, so I went back to Brooker's, waited for the fairground to close that night, and took him home soon after. He was not unintelligent, I found – he'd liked the boys' camp in the war, did some arithmetic there, and knew about *Puzzles and Diversions*. Cyril was, I'd say, the product of natural sensitivity, working-class starvation and nervous debility. He wouldn't kiss. We treated ourselves to baths and listened to the late repeat of the Brains Trust programme on learning machines, with Julius Trentham opining, not implausibly in my view, that the human ability to learn is determined by 'appetites, desires, drives, instincts' and that a learning machine would require 'something corresponding to a set of appetites'. And I said something like, 'You see, what I find interesting about that is Julius's suggestion that all these feelings and appetites, as he calls them, are causal, and programmable. Even these things, which we're so sure, so instinctively certain, must be the preserve of freely choosing and desiring humans, may be isolated. They can be caused, and they have a cause.' And Cyril was fascinated. He was listening and nodding. I felt so happy and so peculiarly awful. We went to bed and in the morning I unthinkingly offered him some money. He was offended and left in a mood. I then discovered £3 missing from my wallet – he could have taken it at any time, I put nothing away – and I wrote to him at the hostel, calling things off. He turned up on the doorstep the next day, very indignant, making obscure threats which I did not take seriously. He mentioned an unlikely sounding suit hire debt, for £3 of course, and some other outstanding sums and then ended up asking for another £7, which I reluctantly gave him.

A week later, I returned home from the university to find my house broken into, not much taken, ten pounds from a drawer, some silver plate. I reported the break-in. The police came to the house and fingerprinted it. I also consulted a solicitor in confidence about the possibility of Cyril blackmailing me, and on his advice again wrote to the boy, breaking things off. Cyril subsequently appeared at my house, as before, and this time the threats were not obscure but explicit: he would go to the police and it would come out about the 'Professor' and his chums. We had a row, I mentioned the burglary, and he calmed down and kissed me for the first time, and said that he knew who might have done it – his mate from the Navy. He admitted having boasted of his friendship with me and I was foolishly flattered. Cyril stayed the night and I went to the police station in the morning with some information about the likely culprit and a rather shoddy story about how I'd come by it. The fingerprints, meanwhile, clearly identified Cyril's naval friend, who already had a criminal record and needed little prompting to blab about Cyril's 'business' with me.

The King died in the early hours of the day on which two very kind Police Officers paid me a visit. Seven weeks after my arrest, I was found guilty of Gross Indecency with a male person and sentenced to receive a course of organo-therapy – hormone injections – to be delivered at the Royal Infirmary. The physical effects of those injections have been marked. Almost at once I began dreaming. I do not think deeply about Cyril, it turns out, but about others I think as deeply as anyone can.

★

Things seem to be sadly lost, put to bed, left on top of golden summits in the past, trailing away until we see what the lines of event and memory have traced: a plane. A loop that encloses all loss, has no beginning and no end.

★

I wonder about the coming together of events and people that have produced my crisis. If I were to find a mathematical or topological analogy, I suppose that it would be 'tessellation' – where the contours of one form fit perfectly the contours of another. If I had not finished the paper on morphogenesis when I did, I should not have ventured out in search of a reward. If I had not had the upbringing I did have, I should not have thought of sexual relations as a candidate for 'reward'. The very interesting Mr. Escher, whose prints have finally awoken my fellow mathematicians to the possibility of an aesthetics of undecidability, has called this coming together the 'regular division of the plane', but it is a little more than that, because it is a division that entails change. The world is not atomistic or random but made of forms that interlock and are always interlocking, like the elderly couple in Ovid who become trees. Time is the plane that reveals this interlocking, though time is not discrete. You cannot pin it down. Very often you cannot see the point at which things start to come together, the point at which cause generates effect, and this is a variant of the measurement problem. It must also be akin to asking at what point we begin to lose consciousness when we are given an anaesthetic, or at what point unconscious material becomes conscious. Where does one cross over into the other? If the tessellation of forms is perfect, do they divide? Or are they one?

★

In the third century of the Roman occupation, people buried money for safekeeping, so wary were they of political instability and the possibility of tribal insurrection. Favourite burial places were woodlands, the natural shrines of outcrops and waterfalls; springs and high ground. I read of this in Jacquetta Hawkes's invaluable history of these islands. The Romans borrowed the traditions of the late Iron Age natives and burying wealth became not merely a rite of propitiation but an act of generosity, not a symbol of something but a self-contained reality, as important as the giving of oneself to the day, every day. Into the ground they went – bags of coins, silver denarii, gold solidi, pots of chaff, figurines of fauns and satyrs, phalluses, antlers, votive objects, brooches, spearheads, bridle rings, weapons and shields, and cauldrons of course. The cradle of the feast. It is difficult, after the cataclysm, to retrieve one's thinking at the time, but when war was declared I, too, amassed my savings, or a goodly chunk of them, and bought two silver ingots and buried them. I did not find them again. I have them not, and yet I believe that they still exist somewhere and that they are of value. The evidence is lacking and I appear not to be interested in the evidence after all: my belief is that I have lost something of value. If only we could believe we were just carbon and water, we could leave life behind very phlegmatically, but belief gets in the way. Because: what is belief?

★

Living on your own makes you more tolerant of people who say strange things. I met a dog-walker on the Common recently who greeted me as I rounded the bandstand as if I were a close friend returning to her side after a trip to the toilet. She looked over the misty grass and said casually, 'This is where I scattered my father's ashes.' I suppose she was in some sort of pain. Pain is the invisible companion. At the fairground, where I met Cyril, there were the remains of freaks – strong men and a boxing booth with a poor giant of a man soaking up the most dreadful punishment, but also a woman with hyperextended limbs. Freaks live in pain, as do most sporting types and ballet dancers. So much of real life is invisible.

★

These are notes to pass the time, because I am in a certain amount of discomfort. I suppose it is fear, and keeping a partial journal distracts me. But I am also drawn to the pulse of that fear, a beat, an elevated heart rate – and something more than that, which comes through the thinking and is a sort of rhythmic description of my state of mind, like someone speaking quickly and urgently on the other side of a door.

I know that Pythagoras is said to have delivered his lectures from behind a screen. The separation of a voice from its origin gave him a wonder-inducing authority, apparently. Perhaps he was shy. Or ugly. Anyway, I've never had this experience before. This morning I could hear the inner murmuring accompanying trivial actions: 'I'm up early, it's dark outside, the path I laid haphazardly with my own hands is now a frosted curve. I put some crumbs down for the blackbird singing on my neighbour's chimney pot. Beyond my garden gate a road, beyond that fields speeding away towards the tree-lined hills and crocus light. I wait beside a bare rowan, its berries taken by the blackbird and her brood, the wood pigeons and jays.' And then again, moments later, when I caught myself looking back at the garden through the doorway: 'He passes through the silent streets, across wet roofs and closed faces, deserted parks. He moves among the trees and waiting fairground furniture.'

The error is supposed to be 'looking back', isn't it? Poor Orpheus, etc.

Of course, it has occurred to me that the

balance of my mind is disturbed, just as it has occurred to me that I am reckoning with a deliberate retreat from the world, a passing out of sight into, well, invisibility. What lesson might that passage have for me? It is an extension of my preference for anonymity, I suppose. It is commonly said, or felt if it is not said, that people respect others of importance who have achieved things or held office; but it is a curious fact that self-respect is often found to exist in inverse proportion to public status. It has learned to pass nights alone. It does not seek approval because it knows that estimation has nothing to do with achievement.

★

Though it is doubtless an impolitic thing for a materialist to admit, I cannot help wondering if the real nature of mind is that it is unencompassable by mind, and whether that Gödelian element of wonder − at something we know we have, but cannot enclose − may not be the chief criterion of consciousness?

★

There is a picture book in the Royal Infirmary waiting room. I think it is an attempt to improve me, or to give the sickly reasons to get well (art, culture, all of it waiting to be appreciated!) should medicine struggle to oblige. It contains a reproduction of Poussin's 'The Triumph of David'. I was struck by the painting, which I did not know. In particular I was struck by the fact that the young Israelite and the waxy outsized head of Goliath, the slain Philistine, wore similar expressions. They seemed sad, as if they had glimpsed, beyond the immediate joy and horror, echoes of the act in history – its wave-like propagation of revenge.

*

A gardener, today, laying out the Common beds for the council: 'A whole mob of crows died in the meadow a few years ago. They did autopsies, because it was such an unusual event. But they died of old age. They were about seventeen.'

Christopher's age.

*

That life has arisen on this planet might be regarded as a matter for amazement. That it should arise on many others would be, on the face of it, if true, even more amazing. The repeated escape from, as Schrödinger puts it, 'atomic chaos' would be not just one sense-defying statistical fluctuation but a whole series of them. It would be like throwing handfuls of sand into the wind and finding, when the grains are settled, tiny replicas of the Taj Mahal, St Paul's Cathedral and the temple complex of Angkor Wat upon the ground. It would be very lovely, but unlikely. Luckily for us, however, the statistical system of the universe has about it a very marvellous impurity, which is that it functions also as a dynamical system or mechanism for the maintenance and reproduction of order over long stretches of time. Or, to be disappointingly precise, the prolonged illusion of order, because the statistics of thermal disorder are all still there in the background and, like suspicious tax officers, they will get to us in the end. The art of living then, on this view, is simply that of defying them for as long as possible, until equilibrium, which isn't as nice as it sounds, is restored.

★

The alarming truth is that you can't grasp your own condition, though you suspect that something is wrong. You see yourself on the edge of a black hole, or a bowl, or a cauldron, whereas, in reality, you have disappeared down inside it.

★

You know your social life is in trouble when you spend the evening reading an article on puzzles called 'Recreational Topology'. I don't have any kind of social life. It's topologically invariant under many deformations, you might say, although probably only someone without a social life would bother to say that.

★

The other part of my rehabilitation, or punishment, or both, consists of fortnightly meetings with a psychoanalyst, Dr. Anthony Stallbrook. I have approached this with circumspection. I find, however, that it is not as I had been led to expect. He is a most sympathetic, comfortably tiny person with fuzz around the ears and a pate that shines like a lamp in his study and lights the way to two armchairs. No couch. We chat. We go for walks and trips. We are not supposed to go for walks and trips, but then he does not believe in his assignment, that homosexuals require any rehabilitation, or that there is time to be lost where friendship is concerned. Neither does his wife. We are planning a trip to Brighton. Our sessions together founder somewhat on the reef of his presuppositions: I have searched my conscience for repressed feelings and find none. I loved Christopher and had fantasised about a future that involved us living and working together. He took me seriously. I am quite sure that I never fooled myself into believing that he felt intimately about me as I felt about him. His friendship would have been enough. My fantasies were outrageously Platonic, and I have never stopped loving him. At the same time, I am haunted by his presence, molecular, gaseous, call it what you will – and the nearness of his voice and person, on the lip of conscious experience, is a constant anxiety made worse by my own changes. He is as near to me as I am near to the person I used to be, and both persons are irretrievable.

Dr. Stallbrook often asks me how I feel. I reply that I do not know. How *does* one feel? It is one of the imponderables. I am better equipped to say *what* it is that I feel, and that is mysterious enough. For I feel that I am a man stripped of manhood, a being but not a body. Like the Invisible Man, I put on clothes to give myself a stable form. I'm at some point of disclosure between the real and the abstract – changing and shifting, trying to stay close to the transformation, not to flee it. I have the conviction that I am now something like x – a variable. We discuss dreams, and in the course of these discussions I have come to see dream figures as other sets of variables. How else should one account for the odd conviction we have in dreams that the strangers we encounter are 'really' people we know?

What gets us from one expression of the variable to another?

There is a leap from the inorganic to the organic. There is a leap from one valency to another, and there is a leap from one person's thought to the thought of others. The world is full of discrete motes, probabilistic states, and gaps. Only a wave can take us from one to the other; or a force or flow; or perhaps a field. When I look in the mirror, I think, thrice, 'Is it me? Is it not me? Is it not me, yet?'

Dr. Stallbrook encourages me to write. It is like making a will, he says – eminently sensible.

If you've signed your papers and made a will, you know there will be an end. You have already witnessed it, so to speak. And people who make this definite accommodation with their end, with the prospect of death – who get it in writing – live longer. He says this with a matter-of-factness I can't help liking.

★

Julius and others belabour me with questions about thinking machines and the parallels between chains of neurons in the brain and the relationship of the controlling mechanism to output and feedback in digital computers. I want fair play for the computer, of course. I feel, as he does, that 'understanding' in a machine is a function of the relationship between its rules. Recursion may turn out to be reflection in both the optical and philosophical sense of the word. Who knows what machines may end up 'thinking'? But I am privately sceptical of too wide an application of the personifying tendency. One knows oneself to be aware and infers from others – from behaviour, yes, but also from the body or the instrument that produces the behaviour – that they are similarly cognisant. One can't go on from there to supposing that awareness itself is necessary, however. Hasn't it struck most of us at one time or another that much of life is a pointless algorithm, an evolutionary process without an interpreter. On a smaller scale, too, a process such as simple addition has human 'meaning' only because I am there to observe it and call it 'addition'. And yet it certainly happens. Perhaps the larger process, too, is unmeaningful. If life works, it works. The character of physical law as it extends to biological material is that it should underpin the way cells and systems operate, and that is all.

That sounds pleasingly final, but it won't do. I know that. Things don't always add up. I can tell you that it is asymmetrical motion at the molecular level that picks out an axis for patterned development in a sphere of cells – that turns a sphere into an embryo – but I cannot satisfy the person who goes on asking 'why?' That person is the half-wit in a public lecture. That person is a child. And that person is also me. The Church says: 'People come in search of meaning, and to have their fears and anxieties allayed.' But to think you can be finally satisfied on these points, or to imagine you can satisfy others, is the source of the misgiving.

★

I have this strange idea. Christopher left school without saying goodbye. His parents came to pick him up and I saw them get in the Daimler. I was in the upper gallery, working on some diagonals. I looked askance, through the window and there they were, thanking the headmaster, hurrying away. I heard no more from Christopher or his mother, with whom I imagined myself friendly, until the notice of his death. I had not known he was consumptive. He had cold hands.

This is the idea. We, Chris and I, were reprimanded for scrumping apples from the trees that overhung the chaplain's garden. They belonged to Fowle's fruiterers. We were punished and interviewed separately. I think he was told to avoid me. I think he was told no good could come of our friendship, because of what I am, or rather, because of what, then, it was suggested I would become. I am not effeminate, but I am mannered. I am a homosexual, and I suppose that much was clear to the masters. In particular, I think it was impressed on Chris that some polluting disaster would befall *me*, and if only he had asked 'why', my future ghost might have told him.

*

Dr. Stallbrook makes many notes as we go along, talking and arguing, and it has crossed my mind that patients of different stripes must react differently to this. I confess I find it irritating. I do not like being 'marked', or having my papers tampered with editorially, or submitting to a 'clinical' opinion I am not in a position to check. (I was displeased when I found out that I had been circumcised.) And if his notes are, as he claims, 'for his eyes only', then they are unfalsifiable. They may well proceed from a psychoanalytic theory. But how is the theory being tested or controlled? How can it be said to be scientific? He is unflappable, of course; it is not that kind of theory, he says; it is, rather, *theoria*, from the Greek, meaning 'contemplation'. The look of point-missingly clever satisfaction on his face! Anyway, he is not telling the truth. I am a criminal. He is writing reports and sending them off.

The whole premiss is childish, like the schoolboy who covers his work with his elbow to prevent his neighbour cheating. I told him this.

'I'm really not trying to hide anything, Alec,' he laughed. 'I just don't think you'd benefit from reading my notes. My job is to help you *encounter yourself*.'

I replied, in a bit of a torrent: 'Balls. This is passing the buck. This is what my father saw in India all the time – Europeans waving their hands and saying, "but the unrest is *native* and has nothing to do with us". You are not an impartial observer,

Dr. Stallbrook. The observer is a participant, as the great revolution in quantum physics has taught us. Consider now that I am the set of notes that you wish to read. I might as well ask: how are you to benefit from reading me? Shall we condemn ourselves to solipsism? The two sides of an equation must meet if they are to balance. You are dodging the issue. What you want is for me not to press too deeply, not to ask for things you cannot give, not to question your authority. And that is unfair.'

'What do you mean?'

At this point, I lost my temper. 'The assumption of science is that things are discoverable. Things that belong in problems of logic that are not in principle resolvable, belong in a separate category. Things that do not admit of rational argument in another – God, for instance. But things that are just hidden, or powers that are reserved for no good reason because someone 'says so', are the work of the bloody devil! They are a cryptic burden to us all –'

I was half out of my chair, and sat back heavily, because I'd come upon one of my own restrictions and couldn't believe I'd hidden it so effectively from myself.

The Act constrains me, of course. Aspects of my working past are always to be concealed from Dr. Stallbrook. With the result that I am confined to addressing my personal life – aspects of which are presumably concealed from me.

Noticing my discomfiture, Anthony asked me what I was thinking. He sounded very kind, and I wanted to equal him in co-operation. Whenever I have not been able to persuade someone, I have tried to co-operate. I take this view even in respect of my conviction. One should meet bad manners with good grace.

'I'm sorry,' I said. 'I respect a necessary authority. But I do not like dodges or masquerades. Puzzles, yes. Masquerades, no.'

'Is this a masquerade?'

'No.' And I was sullenly silent for a while, thinking distractedly and angrily that civilised England is a masquerade. The War Room is a masquerade when the real thing is far away. Psychoanalysts are doubtless persons of integrity, but persons of integrity may still be pawns. There is usually some rule governing our voluntary actions that we either do not know about or are unwilling to acknowledge – the motives of the companies that pay our salaries and ask us to do things, the real function of justice, and so on. 'No,' I continued, 'but this is nevertheless a *game* with prohibitions we are playing, and one in which you have the advantage. Your opinion of me counts, whatever I say. If you were to decide that I constituted a danger to society, you could have me locked away in a mental institution. But I cannot affect what happens to you. And the further disadvantage to me is that there are things I simply cannot tell you, because I have given my word to others – others in authority – and even the confidences of our arrangement shall not tempt me, because a secret is a personal vow of custody. It cannot be handed over to someone else for safekeeping. And now you will think I am being unfair, and even obstructive.'

'No,' said Dr. Stallbrook, carefully, 'that is not what I think.' We brooded for a while, and the tension eased.

★

Also: just because something is discoverable doesn't mean one has any idea of how the discovering is to be done. One experiments, and sometimes there is a breakthrough and sometimes one has to admit defeat. How is one consciously to encounter one's subconscious? The gap is unbridgeable, it seems to me.

Love is a gap. I used to look at Chris while we were tinkering with chemicals and I'd carry on a conversation, adjusting retorts, making notes, apologising. Thinking all the while: this must be possible; clearly it is, for others manage it. But how?

★

Tolstoy's accounts of Borodino and Austerlitz show us what real war is like: no one knows what the orders are or who is winning. No one has any idea what to do. Soldiers are permitted to kill each other and are maddened, sooner or later, by the realisation that someone else, somewhere relatively comfortable, thinks this is the right thing for them to do. And we are not so far from that kind of chaos in everyday life, really. I walk down the street towards the Infirmary, every Wednesday, and I go in and wait and sit down and everyone is quite polite, and I am played with by the law and turned into a sexless person. The most extraordinary thing is done behind a nice white screen. And the nurse who injects me does it with a good will, because she has been told that it is her job. She doubtless thinks of herself as a freely choosing agent. She likes to think she does her job well, but at the same time she is *just doing her job*. (One hears this a lot.) That means she does not take ultimate responsibility for her actions, because those kinds of decisions are taken, or absorbed, by more powerful persons, like Tolstoy's generals, who know what they are doing. She sees no contradiction between this and her own intuitive sense of agency.

She goes home to her parents' house and has her tea. They have put up some new frieze wallpaper with a ribbon of classical-looking dancing figures where a picture rail might have been. It looks pretty and I wonder how often the family has looked at the actual figures in the frieze, copied from vases in the British Museum by some impish and bored designer. The figures are a) playing music, b) killing their enemies, and c) engaged in exotic but mechanical sexual relations.

We agree not to look. It is a simple but profound contract of the collective subconscious with the truth. If you speak the truth, or do something which indicates how human beings function, regardless of the law, regardless of moral superstition, then people will turn against you, and you must never underestimate how fearful and weak most people in a large body, like a government, or a university, or even an office, actually are. Once you have been isolated in this way, you can be dismissed.

★

I wish people who believe in God could believe in him a little less fervently – could see him as a metaphor for the boundedness of our physical existences and the problem of the mental, which is physical too, but perhaps in a way we don't understand.

★

'You're doing tremendously well!' or even 'you're looking well on it' means: 'Please don't tell me any more about your plight, but instead reassure me that I don't have to worry about this.' Similarly, hilariously, 'We know what it's like. We've just had the most awful trouble with...' means: 'We are not going to help you.'

But they are helping, my neighbours, and I am cruel. They want me to teach their son chess. He is a pleasant little chap with no aptitude for the game or calculation in general, and I suspect that he likes the barley water at the end of our lessons most of all. He stumbles over my name, and speaks inaudibly, which I find upsetting.

*

Doctors can be terribly self-important without realising it because they get to point and diagnose, and if they're pointing at you then of course that means you're not pointing at them. Pointers are an odd lot. They want the triumphant power of clarifying something, of accusation, but they're also jealously private. They don't want to be pointed out themselves: it's a sort of nightmare for them, which leads to them pointing at others more and more often, more and more vehemently. I tend to do it when I get cross. It's an extremely unappealing habit born of heaven knows what guilt and insecurity. But I don't do it so much now – now that I've been pointed out once and for all, as it were. Perhaps I've realised I just *don't* feel guilty of this so-called crime. The whole thing is… pointless. It rather frees one up.

Stallbrook is at least intelligent. The endocrinologist at the Infirmary told me, 'These are conservative measures. The hormone is effective rather than strong. There shouldn't be side-effects.' It is effective, but in a way that doesn't have effects.

★

I liked the Fun Fair and Festival Pleasure Gardens, but I love the old fairs more.

At the Festival there were approved attractions – the tree walk, the water chute, the grand vista, the Guinness Clock, and a marvellously eccentric children's railway, designed by the Punch cartoonist, Mr. Emmet. This last innovation had a locomotive called Nellie, with an engine sandwiched between a pavilioned passenger car and, to the rear, a copper boiler surrounded by a wonky fence. Britain on the move! A weather vane sat on top of the boiler, and a whistle in the shape of a jug. Everything seemed thin and elegant, a series of wiry protrusions, like an undergraduate. The whistle itself adorned a chopped-off lamp-post and a dovecote. It presented an unconscious picture of bomb damage and higgledy-piggledy reconstruction.

Oh, but it was lifeless! In the Hall of Mirrors, for example, I noticed an absence of the laughter one encounters on the seasonal fairground or in Blackpool or Brighton, on the Pier. Instead one had the sense that, in looking at themselves all bent out of shape, people were being reminded of what was not quite right about their day out as a whole, which was that the jollity felt forced, and polished up, and that the element of lawlessness that is so necessary to a carnival was missing.

As it happened, just up the road, Brooker's fair had come to the Common, as it does every year, and that was a proper raffish fair of the old type, with stalls and toffee apples, and fish for prizes, and overcoated old ladies in the payboxes of the dodgems (and the gallopers and the chairoplanes) keeping an eye on the hordes, and gaff lads riding the Waltzers, and duckboards underfoot (the Common has marshy spots), and caravans, and lights everywhere, and yes, the fighting booth, with a few rather tragical looking curiosities no longer called freaks but 'Wonders of the World'. In fifty years' time, you will have my machine in a booth, of course; or better yet my test, and instead of the sign outside the booth saying 'Are you a Man or a Mouse?', it will say: 'Are you a Man or a Machine?' (And the answer will be: both.)

It is an erotic place, the fair. Everything about it – the mushrooming appearance, the concentration of energy, the scapegrace hilarity, the ambush and occupation of common land, the figures moving in the trees after the covers go on and the lights are out – bespeaks the mortal. This is your chance, it says. Take it!

He was wearing a very threadbare black suit, with a grubby white shirt.

The girls, away from their concerned mothers, were hanging about the novelty rides with the flashier gaffers, the ones with studded belts and rings on their fingers and satin cuffs on their shirtsleeves – the ones with sideburns and cowboy swagger. They are not handsome, these lads, and they're filthy dirty from all the putting up of rides and maintenance, but their attraction – to the girls – is their daring, the way they leap about the tracks, hitching rides on cars and leaping off again, and of course the fact that they do not have to be introduced to anyone.

But I preferred Cyril, who was dressed, as I say, in a suit, who seemed shy, and said 'Thank you, sir' in a soft deep voice when I handed over my money. He didn't quite belong with the other gaffers, which meant he was a new hire and not formerly known to the Brookers. And he had a moment's uncertainty – I caught his eye – when he counted out the change and saw that I knew what he was doing.

The double-spin – the spin within a spin – of

the Waltzers prompted me to think about the n-body problem and waves of chemical concentration in a ring of cells, so I was happy to pay for another ride. Well, that wasn't the only reason. This time he gave me the right change and a smile. I took a risk and said: 'I'd like to know how that is done.' 'How what is?' he replied, frowning, and moved on to the next car. But I waved when I got off and his grin was a flash of mixed emotions.

I gave him lunch, which he wolfed down, and we talked. I don't think I expected him to respond to my weekend offer. Asking for things entails a loss of esteem, but he didn't absolutely say no and so I concluded he had been embarrassed rather than put off, and I went back a few days later and loitered.

Though these assignations do not last long, the moment invariably spreads out.

The first thing he did when we met in the trees, in a small bower of hawthorn, was to pick a spiny twig out of the way and thread it safely behind a larger branch moving in another direction. That meant he could then lay his head on my lapel and put his hands on my arms, as if he were bracing himself for something. The tender contract signed, we went about our business very efficiently – Cyril eagerly taking the woman's role, as men least willing to admit their taste mostly do – and the mood changed. The reward for competence is suspicion and, between men, a ruthless brio designed to break the bonds of troublesome affection. Luckily, I am not jealous. 'I want some more,' Cyril whispered to me. 'You can watch if you like.' So I did. He slipped from our shelter into the main clearing and soon found his way, turning jauntily as he walked – almost skipped – to another tree-fringed island where a group of men from the caravans took turns with him. One of them stuffed a handkerchief in his mouth. Cyril turned his head, all eyes, mouth filled up with dots, to look at me while this was going on, to see if I was still there, to see if I was shocked. I was fascinated, of course, and pleased he was enjoying himself, but concerned in a different way. His legs looked thin and white and unfinished with the trousers dropped about his shoes, like the bones of a more robust ancestor.

When the men were done, I went over and asked Cyril if he would like a bed for the night, and he was polite and gentle again, and said yes, that would be lovely. We listened to the radio, as I have said. He told me several of the riding-masters went with lads and that it was one of the perks of the life. He said that there is usually one who becomes the 'dolly tub', a term Cyril did not like, and that sometimes it was very good and others it was too rough and a worry. He would not admit to prostitution and so I made the mistake with the money, which is perhaps why he stole from me. I think being a gaff was a source of pride.

These are, or were, the contributing circumstances. I view them unsentimentally. It is interesting that I do not consider their rehearsal to be a serious kind of thought. Underneath them run echoes and rills of a different order, however, the inner murmur, and these I take to be true thinking, determinate but concealed.

In the middle of the night, with his back to me, and his skin warm, he explained how the short-changing or 'tapping' was, after all, supposed to be done.

'The rich flat' – flats or flatties are trade, the punters – 'the rich flat hands me the money, say a ten-bob note for a half-shilling ride, and I take it to Queenie in the paybox. There's no fooling Queenie, because she can tell who's on the ride, how many, how much should be coming in, so I can't diddle her.' He paused to cough, and I felt his ribs. 'Not so hard!' He settled his head back into the pillow. 'So I collect the change, florins, bobs and sixpences, and go back to the customer, and I count it out from my left hand to my right so he can see it's right: 'Two, four, five, six, seven, eight, nine, nine-and-six, and the ride makes ten'. Now it's all in my right hand, in the palm, but as I tip the coins into the flat's hand, I squeeze my palm, like, to keep hold of a few coins. The ride is running up by this point, so the customer doesn't notice what has happened.' He swallowed. 'Or he shouldn't. It takes a bit of practice. Takes a bit of nerve. I saw you and thought, this one won't shop me. Bit old for me, but not bad.' I could feel his eyes opening in the dark. 'And that's how you do it.'

'I know the weight of the alloy,' I said. 'Two florins and five shillings and sixpence should weigh approximately one and nine-tenths of an ounce.'

'You didn't have to look?'

I said that I liked to trust people, which I do. Lying there, I seemed to float outside my body and look down at us both. The objective viewpoint. I could see him laughing into the pillow, his eyes going right through the wall into the ivy and the street.

The Waken

Jenni Fagan

HER FATHER'S CORPSE WAS staring out over North Atlantic swells. Nobody knew exactly what cliff top. The women only came to host the Waken out of goodness and the men only took his casket on their shoulders to make sure he was gone.

He had fallen with a thud.

In the hallway his long torso paled at the end of huge feet.

His tongue as thick as it was in life.

There was still ash in the fire from where he'd hurled a book into it the night before. Not keen on reading, her father. Not interested in opinions (other than his own), found women idiotic (useful mostly only for cleaning and bedding) and men weak (less-than-himself-in-every-way), and he regularly declared all children to be – total arseholes. His use of language was delicate as his fist and laced with a similar fury. That clunk in their hallway was one of the sweetest moments of Jessie's life.

There is an order to things.

On the island this has not changed for generations.

First things first: open all of the windows so the soul can get out but snap them quickly shut again, lest the soul dare return. Similarly: turn each kitchen chair over so if the soul does find a way to come back there is nothing for it to sit upon (and refuse to move like an unruly spirit toddler) (this can happen) (honestly don't test it); finally throw a shawl (or Disney towel) over any exposed mirror. It doesn't have to be a towel, an old T-shirt will do. Make sure the mirror is completely covered, do not leave a new spirit even a half-inch of reflection with which to lose themselves – they are easily distracted.

Stop the clock at the time of death.

Jessie tipped out the battery and sat their small clock back on the mantelpiece. Their white house was now about as soul-return-proof as it could be. Jessie made herself some peanut butter on toast and surveyed the precise stage-of-ritual she had achieved, in the hour since he'd died. If he had been hovering he would have seen her tip over his favourite walking cane and kick his work-boots out her way. She had selected a good roll-up from his tin, taken three drags, coughed and flicked the rest of the dog-end away.

The nearly-departed are vain creatures.

It's wailing they want.

Incurable grief.

Jessie just sat there, with her feet up, in his armchair – reading a book he loathed for a good half-an-hour before she let anyone else know, would have done nothing for his ego at all!

Spirits are prone to confusion.

The ghost must leave the house. It is bad news for all if it does not do so quickly.

Jessie went outside to paint the front door black.

She found the box of white wooden teardrops (under her old Monopoly board) and carefully stuck each teardrop into well-worn gouges (trying and failing to not get black paint on her fingers) they were the same tiny holes she had pierced for her mother last year *God Rest Her Soul* and her little brother before not long before that.

Within the hour her door had been seen by a passer by and the Bell-crier had been informed and he cried out across the valley.

Seven women left their homes ready to help her cleanse and prepare the body and host the Waken. Jessie opened the door to each of them knowing they were not there for her father but for her – God, and decency.

That is how the cleansing began.

Washing the body was monitored by the eldest woman present.

A bowl of water was brought in.

Cleansing rags.

Rubber gloves up to the elbow (this was a recent thing) and hair tied back, thank you.

Each woman cleansed an area of the body.

An arm.

A thigh, down to knee, lift it up, back of the ankle area, hair soaked flat then left to dry and each woman working in quietude and gravity to the task at hand – each deceased body must be cleansed to begin the purification of a soul. During this part the leg is lifted and a rag is used to plug the receptacle (nobody wants leakage during a several day long Waken); it is unpleasant but it has to be done. Sometimes in the final round of cleansing women would sing over the deceased, sing them across to the other side but in her father's case he is probably just lucky they are not swearing at him (each had more than one reason to loathe the man) the cleansing concludes in silence.

Dead clothes are brought in last.

It's the youngest girl who brings the winding sheets (dead clothes) into his bedroom.

There is a copy of a lambing manual by his bed.

A half-empty cup of tea.

She reminded herself to remove that later on and clean the tea stain underneath.

Jessie looked at her father, his thin eyelashes, sparse brows, the terse lines on his forehead. He had been as cleansed and purified as they could manage. They could do no more. The girl stepped forward and laid down a long set of winding sheets. The sheets were kept solely for this purpose. There's usually a box of them at the back of the church behind the picnic supplies for the summer fete. Each of the women present at the Waken (indeed all across the island) had a touch of silver when she turned her hand to wind the mans skin up in white cotton. Jessie was the only one among them who had not been turned as a child. Most changed at around twelve years old and she waited and watched as the others went into the water but for her it was not to be. Selkies are private and mistrusting. Even here with them in the rituals of passing over Jessie is outside (as her father was) but it is through no fault of her own.

Jessie had thought then of the soup she had made for him.

How he'd smiled when he'd eaten it.

She wished she was one of the many island women who swam in the Atlantic swells among seaweed and lichen and called out to sailors and who knew all the rocks where wood had crashed and splintered. Jessie had no smooth pelt but just as the last winding sheets were placed around her father's pallid legs, she felt two budding nubs rise up on either side of her temple.

A quick hand over her hairline (as if keeping it neat).

Small horns.

Just the tips really.

Her father's corpse seemed to smile in its death-stupor and she had to resist an urge to pinch his tattooed forearm and leave a mark for Satan to see later on, it was not like the women would not do all they could to save his soul – it was only decent to do so but many things in this life are beyond the good and the brave. It was only the beginning of the Dead Days then and Jessie could hear neighbours bring extra kitchen chairs in for the Watchers, they would lay a stack of fresh peat by the fire, onions and potatoes and beef and chicken and flour and oatcakes and honey and cream and raspberries and ale and whisky and tea and her little kitchen would be scrubbed by someone else and preparations for the feasting would already be underway.

'Do you want to say anything to him, Jessie?'

Those nubs on her forehead grew harder and more pointed.

'May the good Lord forgive him so my mother can rest in eternal glory.'

'Amen,' the women said.

'It's time for the kistan, is everyone ready? We

lift him as one into the coffin – take your positions.'

Life and death.

Twin fates.

Women's work.

Each of them had watched these rites being presided over since they were a little girl, and joined as soon as they were able and as one they lifted the great hulking body into the coffin. His arms had folded up as if he was trying to dance and they had to shove them down (it was hard to get a coffin wide enough for a man like that and he'd made this one himself, he'd made her mother's and in fact there was one in the shed for Jessie but she'd be burning that and getting the next boat off this island never to return just as soon as all of this was done and if she couldn't get a boat she'd sail out on that coffin with a few good oars and a cross for good luck) and Jessie had brushed down her skirt after that, trying to remove the feel of his skin from her fingertips – while the smallest girl had stared pointedly at her forehead.

A bonnet.

That's what she'd needed.

An old thing, from the olden days, a quirk of her grief.

Her mother had left one in their hallway as if anticipating this exact event.

It was black so it carried the memory of prior vigils and nobody could comment on that so the

Dead Days began with her wearing a bonnet and the smell of soup and stew, fresh baked bread, ale and carrots and onions and butter on her table from the farm next door. Jessie had to take her shift to watch her father's body as did the others and between them they stopped the devil coming in to take his soul. Jessie had sat in the corner across from his body for two whole hours with a growing worry that not even the devil would want her father's soul. Jessie went back into the kitchen after her shift but had a great sense of dissatisfaction whenever she looked at the freshly cooked food. There was a deep yearning in her for the taste of cloth, or wood. Wanting to rub her head against the kitchen table and butt one or two of the children out the front door.

The shutters were drawn until after the funeral.

It was ideal.

Nobody could see what was growing on her head.

She had known how lucky she was to have others to come and help her do the Waken and none of them were blood relations but they all turned up out of decency to a young girl with nobody left on the island anymore. Jessie was already thinking of the city and imagining what opportunities she might find on other shores. Each member of the Waken watched over the deceased in the final shifts, and they performed their duties fastidiously even though everyone on the island (and most of the surrounding ones) suspected the devil had taken her father's soul a long time ago.

He'd spread his seed among this community.

Fought husbands.

Burned down the village barn.

Teased children.

Kicked bulls.

Spent many nights toasting the lack of police anywhere near these shores.

While the community performed the Waken like the good people they were, it was also a long-anticipated exorcism for this small community. The horns on her forehead had grown longer and sharper by then with a nice curve to each tip. After life with a man who oozed anger and resentment – with his oily mind and spiritual decay – this was a welcome oddity. Outside their family home (which would automatically return to the farmers they'd rented it from for all those decades) the sky was so grey and dreich it was hard to believe summer could ever have visited such a place.

'What kind of a person never cries?'

'You don't, Father.'

'But you are a girl! You don't even flinch! Not even when a man raises his fist?'

Unease.

If a man as horrible as her father could have

been so unsettled by her presence what did that mean for her soul? Jessie had picked her way among the members of the Waken, noting their glances toward her, their worry that she might stay among them and find a boy and seduce him and bear children and bring another male MacCrae back to this island when this one had only just gone.

Jessie had tried to breathe quietly in the kitchen, as if breathing itself were a statement of intent, even among the women it seemed she was stealing air that truly belonged to them. A hard knot at the bottom of each horn on her head had began to burn then. An undeniable itch. One that would have to be fulfilled. Her mother had grown smaller and frailer under her father's sneer and loathing, his fists and his envy – the puerile fascination with disintegration (sheep's heads on the counter, leave them until they bubble with flesh all rotten and blue) she wanted to bring him back from death then so she could stake him with her new ivory horns.

'Are you okay, Jessie?'

She looked up, hoping the bonnet still restrained her true nature.

'I'm fine.'

'We'll start the feasting, there's seven courses, then the men can take him up to the churchyard and lay him to rest, okay?'

So they ate.

Her own father laid out on his bed like a poorly child.

Arthur had been stood just there outside her front door where men had started to gather.

He looked in at her like she should be going home with him after this and as if he thought she was a nicer person than she was and it took all her sense of self to not paw the ground with cloven hooves and run at the men out there. They'd stake her in the heart of course. They'd chop off her head and stick it on a gate at the edge of the valley so she could smile at the tourists who came each year to see this primitive community (to them), to witness how nature still worked, who walked past her home through late September months hoping to see the aurora borealis or the many kinds of eagles, or owls, or even bats swooping by.

She'd never build another dyke wall.

Never dip another sheep in dye at the pen.

She'd not stack wood or mend fences or sit in silence by the fire.

His walking cane had been sat back upright at the door and rage burrowed inside her – wasp-like – the wrath of every ancestor had been borne into her mother directly by her father and the direct outcome of it all was her.

If Jessie could have taken the shawl off her mirror – there would be the faintest tuft of a billy-goats gruff quite visible on her chin but she could not and instead noticed (thankfully) that every one of the men at her front door was more than a wee bit drunk. The women were beckoned together for the First Lift – to rise up as one with the coffin on their shoulders. It was women who eased the passage between the twin rites (life and death).

The women lifted the casket upon their shoulders.

He was heavy.

There was a smell of whisky and pipe smoke and a lightness in the house now he was about to go. They had all done their job. They could sleep well at night. Not one thing on this island was sorry to see him go. The casket was heavy on Jessie's shoulder but the women linked arms to make the First Lift more secure.

They moved forward in time with each other. They took small and steady steps and walked her father out of his home feet first – lest his soul try and come back in. Outside the men took his casket onto considerably broader shoulders and they were off. The procession walked up the hill (the women going home letting the men take the final part of the journey) and Jessie stood in the garden as they faded away towards the church – swaying, arguing. Up at the top of the hill another procession with a different coffin on their shoulders lurched out of the woods and the two parties had began to shout at each other and no doubt a fight would ensue all the way to the church two miles away. The men would stop and build stone cairns along the way to mark the route of the dead. There would be a dram taken at each cairn. The men walked slowly up the hill going around the second funeral procession and she wondered who it was that had died on the same day as her father and she continued to watch from the door as her father's casket got smaller and the sky darker. It was only 3 p.m. but winter was here now, it would be dark by this hour each day.

Waves crashed nearby.

The sea was never quiet. It was always ommitting huge banging groans and always a smell of brine on the air and under that the faint clean-sharpness of whelks and hard pebbles washed by seaweed – if she could have bottled that smell it would remind her of home no matter where she ended up. The women were gone, raising a hand as they disappeared down a sandy path to nearby shores. They'd shed their mortal skin and don fine silvery pelts so they could dive down into the great North Atlantic ocean swells – each of them whiskered and able to swim so easily it must feel like they were flying. Her father's toenails were thick and yellowed. Her last memory of him will always be that horrid naked flesh. He could at least have got dressed before he dropped down dead but it happened too quickly for that – here – thud – gone!

The evening arrived to clear out the old minutes from the day, punctuating the sky with stars and a fine thread of a moon. She took her bonnet off and stood out there just to feel the night and her new freedom and she was still in the garden when two men stoated back down the hill.

'They'll never find him.'

'You were all too busy swooning over the seal wives.'

'Their singing!'

'Who knew they'd be burying someone from Blacksheep at the same time. Starting a fight with two corpses on the shoulders of different sets of men! It is an undignified way to lay to rest the dead.'

'That's what you were saying with your fists was it?'

The men were laughing.

They stopped at Jessie's gate and one lit a cigarette.

'Nobody is going to find him, it's a cliff and there was sea and a moon, take that as pointers! MacCrae will be gazing out over the Atlantic until he turns into a skeleton.'

'Well, bad men deserve to be eaten by goats, that's what I say.'

One of them had unlatched the gate.

Jessie had stepped forward and the two men

had been unconcerned as she clopped out over the stones. A surge of power in her forelegs. She had cantered forward easily. Skipping without breathlessness across the stony ground. Autumn had left the grasses balding. Winter had arrived on the island that day. Jessie climbed down a cliff that was almost vertical – with no difficulty at all. There was a half-splintered casket far below on the rocks. Waves coalesced into a foaming mass. If she tipped her father's body forward just a half-inch forward he would have fallen on those rocks. The sea would take his body and it would bloat and turn black. Jessie had no desire to taint the waters of seal wives or seahorses, nor migrating mackerel or killer-whales or wide-hammer sharks, she would not force such a corpse on the sea-kelp or algae, or plankton – nor sully the magical sparkle of phosphorescence that glittered so prettily under a winter moonlight.

He was not worthy to be dragged along the seabed.

Jessie's hooves took hold in the rock. Firm. Solid. She was barely moved by the wind beginning to batter off the coastline, spraying sea foam up into the air. She nibbled at the first winding sheet with relief. This is what she had been wanting. Cotton. A good grain to it. It was so easy to chew through the material and it had some bite and substance as she swallowed it down. Her long front teeth protruded forward – she could eat an arm through a letter-box with teeth like this. Her father no longer appeared to be smiling as he looked out across the ocean. There was sea spray on his eyebrows and his expression was one of uncertainty. He had looked a little like that when he'd went for a nap after his bowl of soup and a similar emotion crossed his face as he had walked liked a great, naked, entitled, hairy baby down their hallway only a few days before and she'd passed him and wondered if it had worked and then the thud on their floor.

Jessie had gazed out over the sea.

It was a certainty in her that by late morning she would return to her other form just as the seal wives and when she did she'd go out there, across the water to the mainland and never return to these shores.

Perhaps she'd find others (as bad as this one) or even worse perhaps.

Her mother would not rest in peace until vengeance was fulfilled. It was her only daughterly duty now. She was the last of their bloodline on this island. Heat rose in the horns on her forehead as Jessie staked him through his fleshy heart and took a generous meaty bite. A boat sailed passed her – as dawn rose – an early set of tourists going whale-watching for the last part of the season. Jessie caught only the faintest of words on the wind *wild-goat-what-has-it-got-can't-see* and a flash of a camera and hoping they clearly caught the blood on her lips, on her horns, that these photographs would go out into the world as some kind of a warning to tyrannical, stupid, lumbering selfish men whose entitlement knew no boundary – the kind (if left unchallenged or without vengeance) that becomes far more fatal and dangerous than any pure evil.

The Edge of the Shoal

Cynan Jones

[Shoal / ʃəʊl/ – noun 1: a large number of fish swimming together. 2: a hidden danger or difficulty.]

HE SWINGS THE FISH from the water, a wild stripe flicking and flashing into the boat, and grabs the line, twisting the hook out, holding the fish down in the footrests. It gasps, thrashes. Drums. Something rapid and primal, ceremonial, in the shallow of the open boat.

Flecks of blood and scales loosen, as if turning to rainbows in his hands, as he picks up the fish and breaks its neck, feels the minute rim of teeth inside its jaw on the pad of his forefinger, puts his thumb behind the head and snaps.

The jaw splits and the gills splay, like an opening flower.

He was sure he would catch fish. He left just a simple note: 'Pick salad x.'

★

Briefly, he looks towards the inland cliffs, hoping the peregrine will be there, scanning as he patiently undoes the knot of traces, pares the feathers away from one another until they are free, and feeds them out. The boat is flecked. Glittered. A heat has come to the morning now, convincing and thick.

The kayak lilts. Weed floats. He thinks of her hair in water. The same darkened blond colour.

It's unusual to catch only one. Or it was just a straggler. The edge of the shoal. Something split it from the others.

He retrieves a carrier bag from the dry bag and stores the fish. Then he bails out the blood-rusted water from the boat.

Fish don't have eyelids, remember. In this bright water, it's likely they are deeper out.

He's been hearing his father's voice for the past few weeks now.

I've got this one, though. That's enough. That's lunch.

The bay lay just a little north. It was a short paddle from the flat beach inland of him, with the caravans on the low fields above, but it felt private.

His father long ago had told him they were the only ones who knew about the bay, and that was a good thing between them to believe.

You'll set the pan on a small fire and cook the

mackerel as you used to do together, in the pats of butter you took from the roadside café. The butter will be liquid by now, and you will have to squeeze it from the wrapper like an ointment.

The bones in the cooling pan, fingers sticky with the toffee of burned butter.

He was not a talker. But he couldn't imagine sitting in the bay and not talking to his father.

There is a strange gurgle and a razorbill appears, shudders off the water, flicks its head and preens. It looks at him, head cocked, turns as it paddles off a few yards. Then it dives again, and is gone.

★

He takes the plastic container from the front stow. It has warmed in the morning sun, and it seems wrong to him, the warmth. As if the ashes still had heat.

He unscrews the lid partially, caught by a sudden fear. That he will release some djinn, a ghost, the fatal germ. No. They're sterile. He throws science at the fear.

He's had to go through so many possessions, things that exploded with memories during the past few weeks; but it is the opposite with the ashes. He tries to hold away the fact they know nothing of what they are. Wants to remind the ashes of events, moments. To make them the physical thing of his father.

After the brief doubt, he relaxes again. Can feel the current arc him out, its subtle shift away from shore. A strong draw to the seemingly still water.

He has a sense, out here, of peace. Thinks, *Why do we stop doing the things we enjoy and the things we know are good for us?*

When he had fetched the kayak out from under the tarp, there were cobwebs, and earwigs in among the hatch straps.

He had not told her he was going. He'd expected it to be a weight he wanted to lift by himself.

There is a piping of oystercatchers, a clap of water as a fish jumps. He sees it for a moment, a silver nail. A thing deliberately, for a brief astounding moment, broken from its element.

*

Round the promontory, he fades the kayak, lets it drift, wiggling his ankles, working his feet loose with arrival. The water beneath him suddenly aglut, sentinel somehow, with jellyfish. He wonders if they are a sign, of some increasing heat perhaps. Then the noise of music hits him.

A child knee-high in the water, slapping at the waves. Another coming tentatively down the stones. A mother changing inside a towel.

The ashes sit perfectly in the drinks holder by his legs.

Laid out farther off, an adolescent girl. The sound of her radio travelling. A pile of bright things.

The child has found a whip of kelp and slaps at the waves.

'It's okay, Dad,' he says. 'We'll come back later.'

The sound of a Jet Ski, from the beach in front of the caravans. An urban, invasive sound.

'We'll come back when they've gone.'

Out in the distance, a small cloud. A white flurry. A crowd of diving birds.

They won't be here all day.

Then he paddles, the ashes by his legs, in a straight line out to sea.

★

It's as he's holding his hands in the water, rubbing the blood and scales from them, that the hairs on his arms stand up and sway briefly, like seaweed in the current.

The birds that had indicated the fish had lifted suddenly. They are faint implications now, a hiatus disappearing against the light off the sea.

He is far enough offshore for the land to have paled in view.

The first lightning strikes somewhere out past the horizon. At first he thinks it some sudden glint. The thunder happens moments later, and he feels sick in his gut.

He sees the rain as a thick dark band, moving in. Starts to paddle.

Then there is a wire of electric brightness. Three. Four. A rumble that seems to echo off the surface of the water.

He counts automatically, assesses the distance to land. Another throb of light. The coast still a thin wood-coloured line.

The wind picks up, cold air moving in front of the storm. And then there is a basal roll. The sound of a great weight landing. A slow tearing in the sky.

One repeated word now. No, no, no.

When it hits him there is a bright white light.

★

He wakes floating on his back, caught on a cleat by the elastic toggle of his wetsuit shoe. Around him hailstones melt and dissipate. They are scattered on the kayak, roll off as it bobs on the slight waves. There is a hissing sound. The hailstones melting in the water.

He stares around, shell-shocked, trying to understand, a layer of ash on the surface of the water. He cannot move his arms. They are held out before him as if beseeching the sky.

Dead fish lie around him in the water.

He gets himself to the boat, the boat to him, drawing it with his leg, shaking until he frees the toggle, turns, kicks, twists, trying to lever with his useless arms. Somehow tips himself into the boat.

Live, he's thinking. *Live.*

His fishing rod on fire upon the water as he slips off the world again, and passes out.

★

He moves because he coughs, a cough made of glass. Slowly lifts himself. One eye closed with salt. His face has been in the floor of the kayak and the salt is from the evaporated water. The sun had come out hard after the storm and evaporated the water, leaving the salt in a crust on his eye. When he opens the other, the light blinds him.

It hurts to breathe because his whole body hurts. As if he has suffered a great fall. His mouth, too, is crusted with salt. He does not know where he is. There is a pyroclast of fine dried ash across his skin.

He blinks and struggles to raise himself a little, the kayak shifting below him. The world slipping, rocking. When he grimaces, his lips split and bleed.

He looks down at his hands, feels the briefest twitch in his right arm, a wave and it spasms, smashes unfeelingly against the inside of the boat and goes dead again, falls against his side, a fish flicking after suffocating.

What happened? His consciousness a snapped cord his mind tries to pull back together.

His left hand stays inert, fractalled with purple; seems tattooed, in a pattern like ice on aeroplane glass.

★

The right arm, for a while, is wayward. Movable, but numb, clumsy.

He does not know how long he has been like this. Who he is.

He sees a rouge burn through the dry salt on the muscle of his forearm, sees the line of his shinbone startled and red. Feels his face. Like something felt through packaging, hears more than properly feels the paper of his dry cracked lips. He has the strange conviction that if he opens his stuck eye he will see what happened.

When he tries again, it's as if that eye leaves his face and flutters by him. A butterfly.

It takes him a while to focus, to accept it. He's forgotten there is other life. It puppets around him.

He cannot believe that a thing so small, so breakable, is out here. A thing that cannot put down on the water. How far must we be from land?

The butterfly settles on the bright lettering of the boat. He watches it open and close its wings in the sun. Opens and closes his working hand.

He reaches up and scrapes the salt from his closed lid, picks at the hard crystals. He wets his hand in the water, blinks with the sting as he bathes the eye.

When he refocuses, the butterfly is gone. For a split second, he believes again it was his eye, then he spots it, heading out over the water.

He feels a confusion, a kind of throb in his head. There is a complete horizon. A horizon everywhere around and no point of it seems closer than another. It brings claustrophobia. He does not know if he's moving – if he's travelling. He cannot tell in which direction if he is.

He feels only the rock, the sway, the dip and wallow of the boat.

★

For a moment, as he lifts from sleep, he thinks the warm sun on his neck is someone's breath. Hears, far off, the sound of a speedboat engine. There is land in sight, like a presence that has woken him.

He wakes with the understanding that the paddle is gone, and with that comes low panic.

His good arm has been in the water, and it is only as he raises it that he feels the little finger has been stripped.

It is torn and frayed to the first knuckle, skinned and swollen ragged with water, the pain searing and hot. The nail is still there but tooth-marked where the little fish have bitten at it. As he touches the finger, his head spins, and when he passes out, again, it's like another white light shoots through him.

★

The thump of the fin stirs him.

His head was resting on the gunwale as the dark fin struck.

He does not move. Cannot move. A few yards off, the fin rises again, a half-metre sail out of the water, a gun-grey body. His primal systems fire a wave of fear through him, the adrenaline trying to get through him like water poured on ice; and the fin folds, disappears.

He is frozen, urinates, cannot move his head.

When it bumps again it is as if the fin has grown tactile. It folds and flops, reaches into the boat, hallucinatory, cartoonish, like a sea lion's flipper. And then the body of the fish, clownlike, lolls side-on in the water, a disk the size of a table.

This cannot be happening, he thinks. The sunfish and he eye to eye, its curious fin folding, flopping. An aberrant ripple to the water in the otherwise lambent calm. *This is it,* he thinks. *This is it.*

★

The sunfish stayed with him for hours. It could be said it steered him. It was almost the size of the kayak in length and bumped and rubbed the boat with a droll

58

instinct, as a cow might a post.

The sunfish is not fishable, not edible, and no instinct has been driven into it to stay away from man. And perhaps it was the warmth of the boat it liked, with the plastic heated by the sun. Or perhaps it was something more.

But it stayed and bumped the boat for hours, and by doing so steered it; and it cannot be known whether it was deliberate, benevolent, that it did not steer the kayak farther out to sea.

★

He tries the screw of the locker in the centre of the kayak, confused by his sureness that there is a first-aid kit, confused given the things he does not know. The locker will not shift. *Focus*, he thinks. *Just accept the pain. Focus on the fact that the land is there.*

He turns in his seat and reaches for the dry bag, husbanding the finger. Uses his teeth and his hand to open the bag and spill out the looser things – the sunblock, the T-shirt, the old cloth.

His ears are blistered and cracked. His skin parched and sore, stretched and gritty with salt. He rubs the sunblock in. A baffling thought of holidays. Works urgently, as if the next few moments are vital.

He rubs it on his dead hand and is frightened. That he cannot feel it. That it lies so inert. He feels a sort of horror at his body. How long has this taken to happen? How long have I been out here?

He looks again at his useless hand, the now fernlike pattern. It seems to follow his veins, mark tiny capillaries, a leaf skeleton disappearing under the tide line of ash into the sleeve of his top.

A wave of sick goes through him.

The idea of breath on his neck lies under everything. A suspicion that someone has been left behind.

★

He takes the T-shirt and wets it, wraps it on his head, the touch of it a heat at first against his burned skin. But then it cools, and there is a sort of weight lifted, as if the sun had stopped pressing.

He unzips the pocket of his buoyancy aid and fumbles out the phone, drops it into his lap as he pops open the waterproof pouch. He turns it upside down and tips the phone out, *thunk* on the boat, picks it up and tries to start it. Nothing.

Take it apart. Let it dry out.

He struggles with it until the back slips off. And there against the battery is a wren feather.

He traps it with his thumb. Holds it carefully. His memory like a dropped pack of cards.

Next door's cat. Its strange possessive mewling, crouched over the wren, the bird like a knot of wood.

The bird vibrated briefly when he picked it

up, a shudder of life. Then flew away.

He could not picture her, but a sense of her came back with that.

They had kept a feather each.

*

Shouts. Faintly. Loud shouts that reach him quieter than whispers. That seem to carry on the air like faintly visible things.

He notes movement, just a shifting of the air, the smallest breeze that bears the shouts; a sure current, the kayak drifts. Goes sideways past the shingle bay.

He is in a dream. He sees, there, a penguin crowd of people bathing in their clothes. In black-and-white suits. They are playing in the water. Children in waistcoats. As if a wedding has run into the sea.

Where am I?

He lifts his arm. They are far off. Tiny on the shore. Tries to shout. Shouts like a puncture. Like a hiss of air.

Hears the draw and swash of the waves breaking in the bay, sees the children jumping the water. The sound of play. A bus parked on the road behind the beach.

Are they celebrating the end of the world? he thinks. *I am dreaming. They are bathing in their clothes.*

★

He watches the land fade, as if it were slowly sinking into the ocean.

He has bailed out the cockpit as best he can. The cloud of dark piss, the tide mark of salt that shows how the water has evaporated.

Scales of mackerel decal the inside, here and there is a zip of dried blood.

The ringing in his head is a hum now, a low choir, the flick of water on the boat constant, random, like the sound of work in the distance.

For a while, as he drifts, it is not the thirst, nor the sun, nor the open space around him that occupies him most. It is the need to stand up.

He tries the locker again. Pressures and turns with his thumb and finger, patiently until the screw hatch jumps and, after a few hard-fought-for millimetres, rattles loose.

He fishes out the built-in pouch, squeezes the toggle and loosens the drawstring.

He unrolls the first-aid bag, the rip of Velcro a strange abrupt noise that seems to tear the fabric of sounds he has got used to. With the violence of the act, some of the dried ash falls flaked from his skin, as if drawing attention to itself.

He opens his mouth – winces at the chapped cracks of his lips – and bites down on a roll of gauze, uses an antiseptic towel on his finger. He even smells the sting, as he did as a child, Dettol on a grazed knee. He rocks it away, humming through the gauze, rocks until he can open his eyes on the pain.

He tears the dressing packet, puts the pad down on his thigh, and wraps it clumsily around his finger. The effort makes him reel. Then he pulls the papery tape with his teeth and gets an end around the dressing, jams the roll between his knees, makes a clumsy bandage. Fits on a plastic finger guard.

★

The water slapping the side of the boat picks up. It's just the angles, he tells himself. It's because I'm shifting my weight.

He leans over the front stow, unclips it, and draws out the large dry bag, sees the small pan in the hold, the rolled cloth that contains cutlery, a wooden spoon.

He feels odd little humpback lurches, an empty sickness without food. He has the bizarre sense that he could reach out, feel the same little kick in her stomach.

He pulls out a carrier bag. It is heavy with a bottle of water and a bottle of dark beer. He stares at the beer for a moment. He was going somewhere. He was going to drink a beer. Then, fumbling, urgent, he takes a drink of water, warm, hot almost, wets his mouth, lips, lets it spill wastefully over his chin. There is a shock at the immediacy of its effect, a voice screaming, *Do not waste this; do not drink too much*. He brings the bottle down with a sort of fear. Don't drink too fast. Remembers watering a dry plant too quickly.

You have to save this, he thinks. Dry dirt will repel the thing it needs the most. Stares again for a moment at the beer.

He empties out the dry bag: Small gas stove. Espresso cup. Coffeemaker. Small plastic box of coffee. Tackle box with traces, hooks, weights, swivels, lures. Thick jumper. Reel of fishing line. Cagoule.

You went out. You went out too far fishing.

He keeps to hand the thick jumper. Tucks the cagoule in by the seat. Takes a brief inventory of the boat. He does not add: One man. One out of two arms. Four out of ten fingers. No paddle. No torch. One dead phone.

★

The sun drops beautifully.

He takes off the buoyancy aid and pulls on the jumper, useless arm first.

He puts the cagoule on, again the useless arm first, but cannot zip it up. Then he puts the buoyancy aid back on, and in the doing of it loses the T-shirt from his head. Watches, stoical, as it floats out on the water. There is a slight swell to the sea now, and the pan and the bottle in the forward hold roll and scrape inside, roll and scrape with the loll of the boat.

He scoots forward, opens the hold cover, horribly aware in that instant how small the kayak is, stuffs the pan and the bottle under the dry bag to jam them.

Of all the things to put up with, that would be too much: the persistent clunking. It is one of the few things he has any say in.

He has a horrible fear of falling out of the boat. Its frail platform. Of being afloat in the coming darkness.

He slips the bungee from the back bay over himself like a seat belt, fastens one end of the paddle leash to the carry handle, the other round his ankle. It is nothing. But it is all that he can do.

*

With dark, the cold hits. It is immediate, comes with a sureness that it will get colder.

For a long time he fights the need to piss. Or what feels like a long time.

The swell picks up. The boat dips, sways as if two unseen hands are shifting it, panning for rare minerals. With his empty stomach, he feels a constant bowl of nausea.

He lifts off the bungee, kneels in the boat, and pisses off the side, a weak stream, a stench he hears pattering on the side of the gunwale. But where it hits the water there is a sudden light, a gorgeous phosphorescence.

When he sits back, he redoes the bungee round himself. That some of the stars on the horizon might be the lights of ships, of land, he can't allow himself to think. Cannot allow himself to imagine the warmth, the food, the safety they would mean. It is better that they are stars.

How long? How long has it been? Is this my first night out? I would have been thirstier, wouldn't I, if I'd been out longer?

He looks. A child awake in a dark bedroom. And, after a while, the stars seem to fade, at first very slowly. He does not know if it is an illusion, but they start to go out, like houselights across a night landscape.

He unwraps the emergency blanket, the silver foil of it speaking with reflected light.

The boat shifts up and down, a lullaby hush.

*

It is cold and it is pitch-black. Blacker when he opens his eyes, blacker than it was when they were closed – a stunning nothingness. He is hardly conscious. And he hears the child's voice. Hears the clear troubling cry of a child.

This is not real, he thinks.

He feels that his heart is slow, his breathing flaccid.

Then comes the cry again.

The cold a complete tiredness. A calm. Like an acceptance of drowning.

I can go now, he thinks. *I've done my best.* He feels passive towards it. He is so cold that if there was any challenge to him he would let it happen, gently yield.

A spray of water covers him, pattering the plastic blanket, falls on him, warmer than his skin, and he opens his eyes, sees the green light, the perfect shape of dolphins playing round the boat.

Somewhere he feels his ticking heart, an engine trying to start. Was he nearly gone? *Was* he gone? The child's cry, close by now, of the dolphin calf, and the mother breaks the water, a luminous green form leaving a figure of itself in the air, bright water dropping, a glow, crashing colour landing, back, into the water.

The calf sounded so human. A baby in an upstairs room.

Stay alive, he thinks.

A bright tail, beautiful triangle.

You have to stay alive.

★

He wakes with a strange specific clarity. Three solid simple things: her, the child, his physical ability. These, now, are his landmarks. The night has left him alive.

He sits up. His skin where it is bare has

tightened. Where he touches there is a fine sand of dried salt.

He is uncertain of it, but he seems to sense something from his deadened arm.

He takes the fish from the carrier bag in the dry bag, and the fishing knife, and puts the fish down on the side of the boat, bringing a hollow gawp to his stomach.

He cuts behind the gills, turns the blade flat and draws it along, feeling it bump over the bones of the spine. The fillet peels off like a flap, the meat changed and cured in the heat.

He chews the fillet, the salt meat of it, then drinks some water, cooled again after the night.

It is not possible for him to believe that he will die, but he begins to fear that he will leave her alone.

This is going to be about rhythm. You cannot control anything else. Just your rhythm. You have half a small fish and four inches of water. If you grow impatient, it will go wrong.

The foily taste of the fish grows as he swallows the water, brings a sting to his mouth.

You have to conserve energy, and you have to be patient.

When he turns round to stow the dry bag, there is the land.

★

'This is just rhythm,' he says. 'You cannot race. You will move the boat only a little, but you must not be impatient.'

He takes off the jumper and folds it into a pad. Then he kneels on it, puts on the buoyancy aid, and picks up the small frying pan as a paddle.

After a few strokes, he gets the boat around.

The pain of resting on his burning shins balances the pain of using his raw finger into a tough holdable thing.

'That's the land,' he says. 'That's everything.' It was a low undulating line. It's all about rhythm now.

★

All of his life he's had a recurring dream: the car leaves the road. It is never the impact that terrifies him, wakes him. His fear comes the moment he feels the car go.

His life does not pass before his eyes. There is even a point he feels calm. But then he sees the faces of the people he loves. He sees their faces as they see him go.

★

The lick came into the waves late afternoon, and with it a wide swell to the water. The clouds now were an intentful dark strip on the horizon and they were incoming, and the breeze came before them, bringing patches over the water like a cat's fur brushed the wrong way. He had continued to paddle on and off. Had thrown up after eating the second piece of fish, and that had affected him.

There was a thin bare moisture in the breeze, and every now and then he opened his mouth to it. Gradually he neared the land. The colours now distinguishable.

It was less easy to bear, having the land in view. He did not think, *If I die you must find someone else*; he could not think that. He felt a great responsibility.

He wanted to make sure she knew how to reset the pilot light on the boiler. Pictured a coffee cup, never moved, the little liquid left growing into a ghost of dust. The note: 'Pick salad x.'

★

He thought at first it was a bag or a sack floating stiffly in the water. It was a fence banner. He turned the boat frantically, the handle of the pan rattling and worked loose now.

Seaweed and algae had grown on the banner, so it looked somehow furred, like a great dead animal on the surface of the water.

He pushed at the fur of algae and it slid easily, uncovered a bright picture of a family car.

There were metal eyelets in the corners and along the edge of the plasticked canvas, swollen and rusted in the water, and as he lifted it into the boat the banner caught and bridled in the breeze, the car rippling.

He scraped the bigger patches of algae from the banner with the back of his knife, then doubled the fishing line and fed it slackly through an eyelet and brought it back, tying it to the cleat where he clipped his seat. He did the same at the other corner.

Then he cut the toggle away from one end and took the drawstring from the hem of the cagoule to give himself a cord. With that he tied the other corners of the banner around the carry handles of the boat.

When he put his feet to the banner and lifted it aloft, the wind caught it with a snap.

He had an idea that the land was a magnet. If he could get close, it would draw him in.

★

The light dropped prematurely with the rain. At first thin, persistent grey drizzle.

He cut the top from the bottle and filled it where the rain ran down the sail of banner. His skin loosened. His eyes stung with salt that the rain washed into them. Every so often he bailed out the boat.

It was a light, saturating rain that pattered sharply on the cagoule he had put back on.

Through it the land was visible and grey. Very sparsely, lights appeared.

The wind now brushed the crests from the waves and it filled the sail, blew a fine spray into the boat.

In the falling light it seemed that a shadow lifted up from the water and went past him. A low whirr of shearwaters. A ghost.

He thought then how, for the time he had been drifting, he had not seen other birds. He had not seen a plane.

What if this is it? What if there has been some quiet apocalypse? Some sheet of lethal radiation I survived. Some airborne plague.

He thought of the sunburn on his body, a momentary scald. Of the butterfly. A sect, drowning themselves in the water. The heat, liquid. Sluicing from the air.

Partly, there was relief in the idea. That he would not hurt them if they were already gone.

He shook the thought away.

The premature evening stars. How she wanted glow-in-the-dark dots stuck to the ceiling of the nursery.

★

When it was beyond doubt that the land was nearing, he wept quietly. The tears went into his mouth.

He lifted the banner with his feet a little and saw the growing details of the land. Then he rested, looked at the picture of the bright car. He could not get it out of his mind that she would be waiting on the beach; the bell of her stomach.

It was only then he recognised the danger, staring at the car: the car leaves the road. I have no way of steering. The land is now a wall.

The light was going. The storm was coming.

He felt it in the water first, like a muscle tensing. He would be better off farther out. If he could stay in the boat. If he could stay on it. Ride the storm.

He could hear now, distantly, the boom of water hitting cliffs. A low echo. The first sound of land.

Hold out. All you need is daylight. You could go in on your own if you could see. Trust the buoyancy aid, trust the float. Just swim yourself in.

He turned, tried to look back out to sea. A dark bank moving in.

★

The squall came in like a landslide, with a physical force.

It cracked into the sail and drove the nose down and he struggled to level the boat, the cockpit filling and spewing.

As the sea picked up, he knew it was useless.

The sign sang and hissed and seemed to bolt from him. *You feel the strike*, he knew now. *You feel the strike coming.*

He cut the cord, sending the banner out like a kite. A bird flapping. Then the line snapped and it ripped free, skimmed off over the water. A car out of control.

He held the carry handle, tried to jam his useless arm behind the seat.

You should have kept the banner. You should have kept it as a sea anchor. It might have kept you on to the waves.

His father's voice was everywhere now, as if he had entered the sky.

There was no control. There was a randomness to the water. As if a great weight had been dropped into it. He was horrified, tried to convince himself they could not see him, that they were not watching.

The back tipped, tipped him, plunged with the whole body of the kayak shuddering.

In the half-light it was as if the boat had been driven into a dark rut.

He tried to press the kayak into the water, to cling on, as if to the flank of some great beast. Tried to lean the kayak into the waves. But the boat went round. The sea was up. An uprushing ground.

He thought of the land, the rock. He passed now beyond any sense of danger to a blank expectant place as he undid the paddle leash.

I do not want the boat to come with me. It would be like a missile.

If a bird the size of a wren can survive in the jaws of a cat.

Trust the float now. You have to trust the float.

The Collector

Benjamin Markovits

1.

THERE WERE TWO GREAT storms that summer. The first came off the Sound and bullied inland up the highways, till the cars pushing through it rattled like fan belts. It knocked the Rooster sign loose at Rooster's Liquour on the corner of Route 16. It cracked one of the panes in Robin Bright's front door and broke into halves the holly trees outside his breakfast window.

The morning after, in heavy uncertain sunshine, his wife took an axe to the stumps just below the splits. (It always shamed him that she was better with her hands than he.) They fell creaking and dragging over an oleanthus bush. Later in the afternoon, she fashioned a board out of yew and nailed it to the tops of the stumps to make a bench. It struck him as cruel, how quickly she accepted the death of the hollies. She said the trees cut out the light anyway. She was glad to see them go.

Every dry morning that summer she sat out on what he called the breakfast bench to drink her coffee. In the summers the oaks filled their arms with green and you could only just hear the traffic on Route 16 and see the empty parking lot outside Rooster's. The second storm ushered in the first of fall and blew down from Canada in a cold clear hurry of leaves and clouds. His wife was out driving when the brunt of it hit and all they ever found was the empty Buick, tumbled into a gorge, and lifted from time to time in the uneven floods.

He didn't believe she was dead for weeks. The fact is, he couldn't account for her arrival when she came. And he couldn't account for her going when she left. But he attributed the same mystery to both. The mystery of her will, whatever it was that made her first desire him and later run out of that desire, and go. They never found the body. The gorge, dry most of the summer, had filled and flowed all the way into the Connecticut River at Killingsfield – which afterwards ran out into the Sound again, and into the sea. Five people died on the roads that night. But the other four bodies were found, and Robin only believed she was dead when it struck him as easier that way, and simpler to mourn.

2.

Robin inherited the house when his aunt died. Or rather, inherited the money for it. He was in his second year of law school at Y___, which he cared for little enough. But when the money fell into his lap he had no plans of dropping out.

The only thing he did care much for was collecting. He collected everything. Rocks, of course, when he was a boy, for starters. He gathered them in his mother's old tin of Twinings Lady Grey. Later, books, new and old, hip flasks, watches, stamps. He bought his first car the summer after his freshman year in college when he picked up a plate of Penny Reds. He found a hanging elbow the dealer hadn't seen and sold it on to a sharper dealer for an extra five grand. So he bought the Buick.

He had no illusions about why he collected. A chubby, pink-faced, puff-chested boy, he had been cruelly named. A fact that didn't escape his classmates. Rather friendless, nor by nature introspective, he liked to fill his loneliness with things. And he liked the fact that acquiring those things often, in a practical way, interrupted his loneliness. Dealers of any kind he got on easily with.

In college he fattened properly and began to lose his hair. He had a fund of bad jokes – he collected them, too. But there was something unavoidable about the intimacies of dorm life that helped him to flourish. Nobody seemed to mind him much. He was the kind of guy they almost expected to come across in college and never meet again. So they let him tag along. Especially when he acquired the car.

Law school, on the other hand, was a different matter. Nobody had any time for him. Robin never fared well around people with ambition. He couldn't advance anyone's cause. As soon as he came into the money, he began looking for a way out. But the house he eventually bought was actually an afterthought to another deal.

3.

Robin drove, clanking and low to the road, out towards D___. To look at a cache of unstamped military letters from the Korean war. Letters home, mostly. Robin, still young and pink, took the slow way through Northford and stopped for coffee at a diner overlooking the gorge where later they found his wife's car. Afterwards, he remembered the diner there and ate heartily at the same place, watching the water steam and diminish rapidly after the storm. Pancakes, bacon, eggs, over easy. Ketchup and syrup and yolk running and sticking together. His colour by this time dirty pale and unhealthy.

The place was an old colonial saltbox just off 16. Almost far enough from the highway for quiet. Painted ochre; dull red bricks rose out of the roof and lost themselves in February sunset. The large plot of land gave way on each side first to scrub then pine and oak. There had been snow on the ground but what was left was wet ice broken to bits. A thaw – and Robin suffered the uncomfortable sweats of a thaw, in his woolly jumper and duck boots.

Nobody answered the front door. Eventually a tall bald man wandered round the side, unevenly, with the one-sided gait of a dog. He wore red-and-black hunter's plaid and had hanging jowls and flaking temples under the last of his hair. 'Nobody uses that door,' he said irritably. 'Everybody knows that.' Then after a minute, 'You'd best come round.' Mr. Wallburgher was his name; a retired history teacher.

Later, when his wife used to say to Robin, 'You've got no interest in the world. No curiosity', he'd point out that cache of letters. 'Oh,' she said, 'that's nothing. I got a box full of love letters you wouldn't believe, all to me. To *me*.'

Mr. Wallburgher sat him down at the kitchen table under a swinging lamp. In spite of the mild February sunset, no light shot through the dirty windows. He took out a shoebox full of torn envelopes. His nails were thick, yellow as old bone, and dirty with garden work.

The soldiers' letters, mostly addressed to women, to wives or mothers or sweethearts, wore their good news lightly. In the handwriting itself. What they really said was, *Look Ma, I ain't dead.* The rest of the news they had to tell was pretty dull. Complaints about the food, wet sleep, dirty stalls. People's names scattered loosely — as if they were words of great subtlety and descriptive powers. Robin was an impatient collector and rarely read everything through, even once. Their unoriginal declarations of love.

Robin bought the lot for two hundred dollars and took out the bills from his back pocket. 'Well,' the bald man said. 'I guess I'm glad to be rid of them, but it seems cheap to me. Yes, sir. How do you price a thing there's only one of in the world? These are priceless individual one-of-a-kind love letters that can't be duplicated. It seems cheap.' He spat a little as he spoke. He'd been chewing walnuts.

Later, as he walked him to the door, Mr. Wallburgher said, 'I guess you wouldn't have any interest in buying the place?'

'You mean the house? What's wrong with it?' Robin looked up; the dark had fallen now, and the eaves dripped and water stung him in the face, so he shaded his eyes to keep from blinking.

'Aw, nothing's wrong with it. Only it's big for an old man and dark in the summer. Then there's the mice and which is worse than the mice, the stray cats. They get up a holler you wouldn't believe. These old boxes are young men's houses. It needs a young man to clean 'em out and fix 'em up. It needs women. Plus I'm running out of space to put things. And I don't want it any more, I don't want it any more. All inclusive.' This was his idea of a bargain and he repeated the phrase. 'I'll sell it to you all inclusive.'

He led Robin back in. Room followed room filled with boxes. Only the kitchen was free of the scent of wet card. You had to pick a path through his bedroom next door between roll-top desks stocked with laundry. Then up the sagging stairs, broad and dark. The kind of place you could forget which part of the building you were in or what you were looking out on.

Some of the floorboards had fallen though. You had to watch your step. You had to watch Mr. Wallburgher's step. There were also various machineries: printing presses, meat cutters, and the like. Rows of duplicate specialty books, brand new. Stacks of envelopes, swollen slightly and curving in the heat of the pipes and the coming spring. Broken furniture, desks, one-armed chairs, cracked mirrors. Anything you could get a deal on, in its day, and hope to sell along at a small profit. Figuring: there's a need for every human thing if you know where to look. Till you stop looking. And the thing just sits there, declining as everything does if it isn't used. As everything does whether it's used or not. Robin thought: you could hide a body here for years and never know. You might never remember yourself where it was you put it.

The garden was bramble. Nothing but bales and wires of it in winter. Muddy fertile lawns stinking of the sump. He thought he could sell some of that stuff on, if he sorted it through. Fixed it. Knew where to look.

4.

Amy Lightfoot came to the door and rang the bell. Bright May morning that might turn either way in the afternoon. Robin was in the back trying to clear space. He spent a great many mornings, with his short arms stuck out at the hip, 'surveying the disaster.'

He was almost thirty now. Two years since he bought the place. Time he got a move on. Cash was running dry. He needed a living; or, at the least, something to sell. The doorbell startled him. Then he remembered: about half a year ago, he'd put an advertisement in the D___ Mercury. Offering storage space for a reasonable fee. He had the kind of patience, it never seemed too late to him for a bet to come good.

Amy was a tall young woman with tough red sandalled feet that suggested no-nonsense. She could just about look down her nose at Robin. She wore a denim vest and too-short black jeans. She was fat in awkward places, her arms, her behind, as if hurriedly put together; but otherwise, slender and attractive enough. Her accent was local, though she'd obviously been away a while.

She'd heard he had a room.

'Well,' he said. It was true, he did. 'You'll have to help me clear it out.'

He took her up to see it. She followed carefully behind, with quick familiar eyes, observing. The printing press. The butcher's block. A large television box, damply sagging, filled only with various used-up light bulbs, blackened at the heart. Piles of uncut books.

'What do you need all this stuff for?'

He tried to sound at his most authoritative. Already the presence of a woman had quickened certain neglected impulses in him. The nerves he felt! He'd almost rather she wasn't there. He'd got used to flat expanses of time, where you could see a long way ahead, and there was nothing to see.

'What do you think I need it for? Polishing my teeth? I sell it.'

'What do you sell? Who buys this crap?' Her voice had a boyish roughness to it, not unfriendly.

The roughness was in fact the friendliness, the intimate grab.

'Well,' – he liked to quote presidents and poets when he could. He had the literate airs of the lonely man. But the tone was conciliatory. He was already giving in to her. 'You can fool all the people some of the time. That's what they say. Everybody needs something. Somebody needs everything.'

She looked round at the room he showed her. The view ran down the garden hill towards the empty road. Wet mud at the bottom rose like water against the level of the grass, shining blackly. A truck passed. They watched it move between the broken shafts of a bucket of second-hand baseball bats on the window sill. 'Not this shit,' she said.

5.

After she was dead, the house noises returned. He hadn't minded them before, but now they suggested to him something lost. That is, something stored, in his keeping, only buried in all the mess. He had it but he couldn't find it, that was the feeling. He almost knew where it was.

Mr. Wallburgher was right about the cats. Amy used to feed them. Here kitty kitty here kittying, bowl in hand, gesturing into the exposed foundations of the house. This kept them quiet.

But now their caterwauling rose up every evening like lamentations, wide and unforgiving, the merciless beseeching of the dead. Robin could have come out into the warm nights with a bowl of dry food to keep them quiet. But he let them cry – let them cry – their crying aggravated and almost fulfilled his yearning for her.

A fuse had blown in that second storm. Weeks later he still had to light a fire to see by. Warm nights in September. The blaze gave more heat than light and there was enough heat already. Fireplaces in every room of the house, some of them big enough to lie down in. He sat on a chair under the chimney-flu and read by the uncertain glow. The fire made him sweat. The sweating relieved him of unhealthy grieving salts and oils.

Finally, he called an electrician in, a tight-faced man, who shook his head, exasperated, gratified. Robin, just for the company, asked him to look over the whole shoddy skeleton of wiring. A thousand dollars later, he packed up and left Robin to himself again. That night, shortly before 4 a.m., before the dawn and the birdsong, an alarm clock somewhere began to ring. Loud, electrically insistent, over radio tunes and ads, and growing louder. Till it shut off abruptly at half past four.

It woke him sweating each time. He slept deeply in spite of, because of, his mourning lassitudes. For another week, he let it ring. Waited patiently till it finished, then composed himself to sleep again, amid the electric fury of the birds. Idly, glad almost of the job to do, he searched in daylight for the clock. He couldn't find it.

It began to worry him. Who was it that had to get up at four in the morning? When? Why hadn't they ever come back to shut it off? Mr. Wallburgher? Mr. Wallburgher's wife? Where were they going they had to get up so early? It was about an hour to the H___ airport. Did they have to catch a plane? Did Amy, when she first came to live in the spare room, forget about it when she moved into his bed downstairs?

Next time it woke him, he seemed to hear Amy's insistence in it. Wake up wake up wake up. Wake up wake up wake up. He tore through the house looking for the sound. Wake up wake up. Upstairs, among the boxes and broken things, going room to room. Twice, he narrowly missed stepping through the gap in the boards and falling to the floor below. The ringing swelled and echoed misleadingly. At last, when he had worked his way into Amy's old room, the ringing ceased. He stood there, red-faced, in a flood of sudden tears.

The next morning at four he began the search again. Glass broke around him, as he pushed his way through. Piles of books tipped and slid quietly. He strained savagely against the heavy iron machines and couldn't budge them.

When he finally found it, under a pair of chairs stacked each way, among loose coat hangers, the digital time blinked up at him angrily. 12.54 p.m. 12.54 p.m. Above, a dirty window showed the dirty light of dawn, growing cleaner at the horizon between the trees. He pulled the plug out by the cord and watched the numbers fade silently to black. Of course, the clock was wrong, had started wrong.

6.

Amy, it turned out, the day she died, had a flight booked out of H___ for Albuquerque at half past two. Two policemen came by to tell him. 'Mind if we have a chat?' the tall one said. An unkempt man, with loose brown hair like Amy's, and his shirt untucked. Robin was stumped. He felt himself losing something he hadn't realised he still clung to.

'I remember saying to her,' he said, 'why you going out in this weather.' The wind had begun to knock the rain out of the clouds. Cold drops, too cold for summer. 'Why you going out?'

'I'm going,' she answered. 'I'm just going.'

The other policeman asked for a drink of water. They didn't even look at each other while he fetched it. 'It's beginning to come back to me,' Robin said, stooping over the sink. 'What she was planning to do there. Visit a high school friend,' he lied.

They asked to have a look round, if it was all right with him. 'Please,' he said brightly, 'be my guest. I'll be glad of the company.'

For another week men came and went through his house. He fixed them sandwiches, cups of coffee. He expected to mind their presence, but in fact it was something of a relief. He said to them, 'A widower's house is lonely twice over.' And it consoled him strangely to see them going through his things. As if the problem wasn't only his. When they gave up empty-handed at the end, and moved out again, he felt vaguely acknowledged. There was clearly nothing to be done.

7.

She worked as a supply teacher for a number of local schools, teaching computers. It was plain from the first she considered him a project. Days off, she mooched about with him drinking coffee and telling him what to do. Her long legs crossed, her voice, instinctively, taking on something of his educated air.

The thought of all that clutter made his heart weak. He walked through the narrow alleyways blocked out upstairs, mapping the confusion in his mind. As if this were a vital, a necessary step. As if he could properly begin when he was through. From time to time, it's true, he managed to 'shift some stock.' A claw-footed bathtub, exchanged for a set of antique dining room chairs that needed reupholstering. More clutter.

Amy offered at last to lend him her computer and explain the workings of the internet. He balked, naturally suspicious of the up-to-date. She said, 'You said so yourself. Somebody needs everything. Now you can find them. They can find you.'

Later, she'd come home to catch him on her bed, bargaining. Wringing his hands to get the blood back in them. His eyes pinched and weak from staring at the screen. But the clutter hardly diminished. Openings briefly appeared, only to be filled, by subsequent packages and signed-for deliveries. He seemed to trade simply with the like-minded. Hoarders who could acquire only if they also relinquished. Once he even said to her, 'I sometimes think we're bartering not goods but space. The only way you can buy it is by selling.'

She said, 'Why don't you throw some of this stuff away.'

He shook his head and looked round her room nervously. The prim, made bed. The bedside chair. A glass empty of water on a book. A warning to him. Just a suitcase of clothes and nothing else. Except for the computer, propped up on her pillow. Except for him.

When she joined him at last in his bed, it occurred to him it was only to acquire a wider license. Over himself, his things, his life. Ms. Lightfoot couldn't stand disorder. Her first rule of thumb was, when in doubt, throw it out. He didn't even know where she came from. He'd never met a woman so free of sentiment.

8.

After she was dead, he tried to learn more about her. He asked round at the schools she used to teach at. A little ashamed, and worse, full of pity, to find people hardly remembered what she was like. 'You got to understand,' a woman once said to him, apologetically. 'The kids keep coming in. We're playing catch-up from the beginning.'

Her hair had the two colours of false wood, dark and light brown. Strands too slight curled in the September heats and bunched, hung charged in the air. He imagined brushing his hand past her head and feeling their tickle. At first he hadn't missed his wife in bed – too tired with grieving for physical pleasures – but now he missed her in bed, too. Her sharp hips like a boy's and her large comfortable behind to fill his hands.

Somebody once said to him, 'She was always real familiar looking. But I couldn't place her. I used to say to her, I know you, I know you. Where do I know you from? All she'd answer was, "I've had a long life. Not much money but a lot of time."'

The secretaries remembered her best. 'She was always bringing in something to eat,' a large black woman, wearing a telephone headset and heavy earrings, declared. 'She was one of those natural motherly kind of women with Tupperware and forks from home and enough for everyone.'

It had never before occurred to him that she was motherly. That she was fertile. Her best care seemed always directed at him, but in rather a spinsterish way. 'I'll tell you something else,' the lady went on. 'There was a kind of troublesome kid took to her straight off. I'm not saying most of them noticed her one way or another. But there was a kind of kid – not a bad kid, I wouldn't say that – but what I like to call, *swimming a little low in the water.* Maybe they lash out on account of that sometimes. She handled them like she knew them by heart. By heart. They missed her when she left. When's Ms. Lightfoot coming back? Where's Ms. Lightfoot at? And I used to tease. You was too much trouble for her. She's gone on.'

9.

Once, drawing blanks, on a whim, he decided to try another tack. If only to justify his visit. Robin liked talking and he didn't often get the chance. He made a point of taking people by the elbow, slapping his knee at jokes. He emphasised all kinds of physical contact. He had an idea of himself that people saw him as a character. He heard them saying behind his back: 'That Robin Bright, he likes to talk.' A little irritably, sure, but also jealous. As if they wished they shared his appetite for words, for passing time. Sometimes, in the long solitudes that followed his casual encounters, he kept up his end of the conversation for days. He liked to imagine what he sounded like in other people's ears.

'You ever run into a fella by the name of Wallburgher?' he asked.

He sat in the headmaster's office on a low couch, roughly upholstered in yellow and brown squares. The headmaster was a stiff-backed gentleman with large hands and knees, consoling each other. He wore a bow-tie and had cut himself shaving. He unabashedly kept in order on his neck the fluttery scraps of toilet paper to stop the bleeding, red and attached at their centres. His manner on the whole was deliberately unembarrassed. As if his lofty position had removed him from the ordinary shames of life.

The school and its history meant a great deal to him. He cleared his throat. Mr. Wallburgher had been an undistinguished professor at their academy for several decades. 'One of those old guys,' he added, lowering the tone, 'you couldn't get rid of. Which I frankly confess it was my job to do on acquiring the incumbency.'

He cleared his throat again and drank deeply from a mug of water on his desk. 'I'm told he started brightly enough,' he continued. 'Came highly recommended from the E___ Academy. If you must know, Mr. Wallburgher had a pedigree we don't often get our hands on. But by the time I arrived he was on the decline.'

I've heard his house gave him a lot of worries. The constant repairs, the isolation. There were questions over his punctuality, of all kinds. Unreturned papers. Misconduct with students. Rumours of an affair or a marriage, later infidelities, desertions. He began to go to pieces and there was nothing I could do. He clung on. Then one day he failed to turn up, unaccounted for. Inquiries were made but nothing came of them. As I said, he had become the kind of man to attract rumours. Not the least of his unpleasant qualities. We never found –'

'I bought his house.' Robin interrupted at last. 'I had some business to conduct with him. Afterwards, on a whim, he offered to sell me his house. And I bought it.'

The headmaster's long fingers fiddled with his bow-tie. 'What's it like?'

Robin considered a minute. 'A full time job.'

10.

Afterwards, on his way out, the secretary apologised. 'Honey,' she said, 'I didn't realise you'd be so long, I should have brought you something hot.'

'So what's the story with Wallburgher and the women?' he said, to make time.

The secretary put two fingers to her lips. Heavily made up, her cheeks had the slightly puddled complexion of a woman who puts on weight and diets in rapid alternation. The flesh was unsure of its tenure. She had the ugliness of a conspirator and lowered her voice delightfully.

'There were different stories,' she said. 'Someone once told me someone she knew knew a gentleman. One of the faculty, a young man, since moved on. Invited home for dinner to Mr. Wallburgher's house. Where he was introduced to a girl he kept chained to his bed. Not minding at all, that was the shame of it. His lover, it turned out, from the last school. A former student. Which is why Mr. Wallburgher wanted to bury himself in these parts.

'But you shouldn't listen to this stuff,' she said. 'It's just school gossip. That's what teachers do, they're terrible. They tell these stories. I think he moved to Florida.'

That night, in his loneliness, as he often did, Robin rummaged through his store of possessions. Looking for the companionship offered by unexpected insights into the self. It occurred to him that what he was doing was rummaging through his own head. Also, that collecting and storing junk was his way of expanding upon the world. Of enlarging the borders of himself.

He found a stack of boxes against a damp wall. They were filled with unmarked school papers. Essays, worksheets, quizzes, often bright with doodles, collages, cut-out newspaper photographs – now discoloured by glue. How quickly these dated. He had a sudden image of the man burying himself under the weight of his inactivity. A difficult, time-consuming labour of idleness. Until he could hardly breathe.

11.

Then the cats got in the house. Often, when Amy came home – it was mostly Amy who used the car, for the shopping, or to stretch her legs as she said, and other unexplained journeys – she gave a little hoot on the horn before she turned off the ignition. This was followed by a car door slammed shut and a half minute later, by the bang of the screen door at the side of the house. Just to say hello again, she palmed the horn. As if perhaps to reassure him she hadn't gone far after all. She'd come back, this time.

Even after she was dead he used to hear the horn announcing her return. The chimneys were wide and the flue leaked air and smoke into the house and the wind sometimes put her lips to the cracks and blew. Hollow fluting tones. They often startled him into getting up: she's back. And he realised how simple an adjustment, in his own mind at least, was needed to restore her to life. To his life. His brain could turn the trick easily.

Once he heard the horn and pushed back his chair at the kitchen table. It was the only room bare enough for him to sit in. He shuffled in his socks to the side door and nudged it open and stood in the doorway, looking out. Mild fall evening, warm under low clouds that broke the light of the streetlamp at the foot of his driveway into arcs and lines. A truck passed by on a low bed of its own sound moving towards Route 16 or the liquour store.

With a sudden electric shriek that stopped his breath, the cats scraped by his ankles at the door. An old tabby. Then a marble-coloured boy, with ugly angry hair. And Amy's favourite, a milk-white cat she called Toothpaste.

He spent weeks hunting them through the dark passages of his attic. Once he startled the tabby in her sleep and almost had her by the neck. But she fell in fright off the back of a bookcase into the intricate odd-angled corridors of his clutter and got away. They had access to corners he had long since given up on. He was almost envious of their bright night eyes and low gait. Such avenues for exploration they possessed.

He slept downstairs and every night he heard the dice-roll of their feet on the attic boards. In college he used to visit the crap tables run by Indians downstate. What lives they led, up there, in those rich nests. Worse than the alarm clock. The thought of them, the noise of them, kept him awake. Those damn cats. Damn woman for feeding the cats.

For weeks he took care to keep all food out of reach, in the fridge, behind cupboards. He washed up for himself straight after meals and left no plates in the sink. He pushed the toilet seats down and kept the taps from dripping – hoping to starve them out, to dry them out. He set pans of food and water on the stoop outside his opened door. But he saw them only in glimpses among the junk, like bright quick fish among still corals. After a while it became clear that the cats had found something to eat. What they ate he didn't like to think.

12.

He let himself imagine what Amy would say to him, by way of explanation. Days could go by, thus occupied.

Sometimes he thought the real clutter was the clutter of days. It was the jumble of them that couldn't be straightened out. Even his few weekly tasks weighed on him like the disorder upstairs. Pay the phone bill. Buy bread, milk. Get a package to the Post Office – something sold. Just one job each day. That was the limit he set himself. But he still couldn't help putting them off. Wednesday, Thursday came round, and the growing anxiety of doing nothing afflicted him like a stifled yawn. Only Sunday set him at ease again. The Post Office shut, the village stores closed early.

He began to drink. He sat deep into the night staring at the computer screen, bidding for collectibles, offering items for sale. Once, on wholesale, he had bought a dozen cheap pipes of rum and a crate of Coca Cola. He opened them now and drank them warm together. To numb him and keep him awake. It became clear to him that he was much worse off than when Amy first came to his door.

I didn't have room to breathe in all that stuff, he imagined her saying. Funny you drowned, he thought, trying to get away. She ignored his crack. In every marriage there's an argument going on from beginning to end, she said. I thought I could win the argument, but I was wrong. It turned out you were stronger than me.

Yes, that's right, he agreed. I am stronger.

At four in the morning, drunk, he became acutely conscious of sounds. He heard the cats overhead, but something subtler, too. The noise of a loose jaw working, the sound of a moth intermittently trapped, unsteady drips, the sigh of a magazine in the wind. He imagined the cats were feeding, their faces wet. He put his palm to his face and tasted the rum wet on his breath, the stale carbonation.

13.

He knew little enough about her. She was raised by her father. Her mother had abandoned her in the early sleepless and loud months following her birth, and long ago, her father said, remarried. In Oregon, perhaps, in the wide corners of the USA. Amy came, she usually explained, 'from round about.' Her father was a claims assessor and travelled frequently, taking her with him on long trips. She picked up a taste for the country. Its variety, its shabby repetitions. And hotel rooms. Their threadbare order pleased her. These were the sweets her youth was fed on. She liked being able to vacate a room she lived in within the hour, leaving no mark of herself behind.

She didn't know she was dying but she knew she was walking out. Maybe she'd left a message. But where? Some place, perhaps, where he could only find it if he had already got the point. A test. But where could he find anything in all that mess?

He spent long mornings and short winter afternoons in the attic, picking over old possessions, seeking evidence of any kind.

He plugged the alarm clock in again and reset the time on the alarm: 12:54. He tried to remember, on the day of her death... Heavy storms had sent him scurrying upstairs with buckets and pans to catch the perfect drum-roll of dripping. Had he heard it ringing? 'I'm going...' he recalled her saying suddenly, 'I'm just going...' He heard the car starting and chased it in his dreams, getting drenched. It wasn't too late to repent. Don't go, don't go, if only you knew. Rain fell so hard on the roof it sounded like the beating of a fist, the crying of a woman. Then the storms in his memory drowned the rest out.

14.

Once he caught his foot on something in the floor, and almost tumbled between the gap-toothed boards. He stooped to feel in his palm the finger-bone tenacity of a young twig, rising out of the cracks. The house was growing again, beneath him. He smelt the green close flourish in the air, so different from the must of old paper, but equally thick. How far had he let himself go? Spring must be coming soon. His life could begin again in the spring. Amy had come in the spring.

Each day, on his trip into town, he let his tongue loose. Shopping for bread, baloney, mustard and Swiss cheese. A newspaper. 'How're you holding up?' they asked him at the till. 'Mr. Bright?'

'What I can't seem to figure,' he began, 'is why I've got so stuck on why she left. It should be enough that she did. That she died. But I keep harking after what she meant to tell me. As if that was the thing that mattered: what she chose to do. As if the whole thing was – I don't want to say her fault – but her willing.' He had an easy amicable air. The colour was returning to his cheeks. He gestured widely with his hands, his mouth often full of a tear-off from the bread.

Always they said, 'I was so sorry, Mr. Bright, to hear about your loss.' It didn't matter what he told them, or the manner of it. Their answers played variations on that theme. He might have said, 'Best thing that ever happened, that storm,' and they would have clucked and nodded their heads and apologised. But he didn't mind.

'I'll tell you the damndest thing. I can't remember anything about the week she died. Except sitting at that diner in Northford, overlooking the gorge. And thinking: I bet I've eaten here before. And tucking in to pancakes, eggs, bacon. How sad and hungry I was. And I remember the funeral. There was nobody there I didn't know. I kept expecting strangers to turn up.

A long lost brother. A boyfriend. A friend. I looked around and thought: I know these people.'

'You sure do, Mr. Bright.'

'I know these people.' But they missed his point. It seemed a woeful thing, to live as she had lived, a wandering life, and leave no one unexplained behind. Except perhaps himself.

'We had a good life here,' he repeated always, waving goodbye. 'That's what I tell myself. We had a good life.'

15.

He didn't notice at first as he sat down on the yew bench. Rooted his bare feet through the loose bark outside the kitchen door. First bright morning in March after weeks of heavy snow. Most of the white was gone. But still its brightness lingered wetly in the dewdrip of the trees and the shining tarmac of his driveway. He set his mug of coffee beside him and stared out at the day. Perhaps there wasn't any message of any kind. Maybe she said to him, the week before, 'I'm going to see my half-sister in Albuquerque. I'll be gone a few days.' She might have said anything to him: he was perfectly capable of forgetting. He only noticed when he felt the streak of hot wet against his pants leg. The cup stood at an angle. The coffee had spilt and was seeping into the red grain of the yew.

The sap of spring rising had twisted the holly bench out of shape. The trees were growing again under their yew lid. Little green twigs had begun to sprout out of the stumps, and the board on top had shifted to fit their renewal. The grain of the yew, once straight enough, had turned upon itself like curly hair. Thin splits opened like mouths around the nails Amy had knocked into the wood the summer before. It wasn't clear the yew could survive. The ends had begun to splinter.

He remembered saying to her, 'How can you cut them down so soon?' He flinched at the percussion of her axe. 'Maybe they'll grow back,' he complained. 'They might heal.' She said she was glad of the light.'

'I thought I was stronger,' she added. 'But it turns out you were stronger.' But he couldn't remember if she'd said that or not. If he'd only imagined it.

16.

Afterwards, when the fire trucks and police cars filled his drive, he tried to explain that he'd been drinking. Pockets of fire still burned. The ochre paint of the old saltbox had crackled and peeled away, revealing first black then red then grey. The windows were the first to go. They popped outwards suddenly in a rush and scattered bright glass on the wet lawn. Then the floors fell through and everything the floors supported and began to burn together. (Whatever was there would never be inventoried or understood. Whatever secrets it contained were now reliably preserved.)

When the windows broke open, the sounds of burning grew louder but clearer, too. He could distinguish a softer tone amid the crashing and roaring. The steady grieving of something that lacked the wit to escape and could only retreat. He remembered the cats. They might scramble as much as they liked now; there were no dark corners. But the keening struck him as too persistent for a cat. It was flat and almost human. The sound of something hopeless nevertheless declaring itself in passing. A lonely exhalation of pent-up breath. But even this subsided when the roof fell in and the walls collapsed on top.

Robin stood back in the road to escape the heat and smoke, which plumed a hundred yards into the spring sky and drifted towards the sea on the breeze. When the air cleared a little, he was pleased to see the charred upright stalks of the trees growing within had survived longest. They lifted their black arms from the ground and would not bend.

He'd been drunk all night with grief and didn't know what he was doing. That was the line he spun, partly true, perhaps. He had to repeat himself several times – they kept asking questions. First in the back of an ambulance, which he explained he didn't need. And later at the police station. Each time different people wrote down what he said. More clutter. But it helps you forget that something actually happened, if you say it enough. After his coffee spilled, he went inside to boil another kettle. One of those old gas stoves you have to strike a match to light. Maybe that was it, maybe that was what he heard – the kettle whistling. He had walked outside, into the fresh green morning, waiting for it to boil.

if a book is locked there's probably a good reason for that, don't you think

Helen Oyeyemi

EVERY TIME SOMEONE COMES out of the lift in the building where you work you wish lift doors were made of glass. That way you'd be able to see who's arriving a little before they actually arrive and there'd be just enough time to prepare the correct facial expression. Your new colleague steps out of the lift dressed just a tad more casually than is really appropriate for the workplace and because you weren't ready you say, 'Hi!' with altogether too much force. She has: a heart-shaped face with subtly rouged cheeks, short, straight, neatly cut hair and eyes that are long rather than wide. She's black, but not local, this new colleague who wears her boots and jeans and scarf with a bohemian aplomb that causes the others to ask her where she shops. 'Oh, you know, thrift stores,' she says with a chuckle. George at the desk next to yours says, 'Charity shops?' and the newcomer says, 'Yeah, thrift stores...'

Her accent is New York plus some other part of America, somewhere Midwest. And her name's Eva. She's not quite standoffish, not quite... but she doesn't ask any questions that aren't related to her work. Her own answers are brief and don't invite further conversation. In the women's toilets you find a row of your colleagues examining themselves critically in the mirror and then, one by one, they each apply a touch of rouge. Their make-up usually goes on at the end of the workday, but now your co-workers are demonstrating that Eva's not the only one who can glow. When it's your turn at the mirror you fiddle with your shirt. Sleeves rolled up so you're nonchalantly showing skin, or is that too marked a change?

Eva takes no notice of any of this preening. She works through her lunch break, tapping away at the keyboard with her right hand, holding her sandwich with her left. You eat lunch at your desk too, just as you have ever since you started working here, and having watched her turn down her fourth invitation to lunch, you say to her: 'Just tell people you're a loner. That's what I did, anyway.'

Eva doesn't look away from her computer screen and for a moment it seems as if she's going to ignore you but eventually she says: 'Oh... I'm not a loner.'

Fair enough. You return to your own work, the interpretation of data. You make a few phone calls to chase up some missing paperwork. Your company exists to assist other companies with streamlining their workforce for optimum productivity; the part people like you and Eva play in this is attaching cold hard monetary value to the efforts of individual employees and passing those figures on to someone higher up the chain so that person can decide who should be made redundant. Your seniors' evaluations are more nuanced. They often get to go into offices to observe the employees under consideration, and in their final recommendations they're permitted to allow for some mysterious quality termed 'potential'. You aim to be promoted to a more senior position soon, because ranking people based purely on yearly income fluctuations is starting to get to you. You'd like a bit more context to the numbers. What happened in employee QM76932's life between February and May four years ago – why do the figures fall so drastically? The figures improve again and remain steady to date, but is QM76932 really a reliable employee? Whatever calamity befell them, it could recur in a five-year cycle, making them less of a safe bet than somebody else with moderate but more consistent results. But it's like Susie says: the reason why so many bosses prefer to outsource these evaluations is because context and familiarity cultivate indecision. When Susie gets promoted she's not going to bother talking about potential. 'We hold more power than the consultants who go into the office,' she says. That sounds accurate to you: the portrait you hammer out at your desk is the one that either affirms or refutes profitability. But your seniors get to stretch their legs more and get asked for their opinion, and that's why you and Susie work so diligently towards promotion.

But lately... lately you've been tempted to influence the recommendations that get made. Lately you've chosen someone whose figures tell you they'll almost certainly get sacked and you've decided to try to save them, manipulating figures with your heart in your mouth, terrified that the figures will be checked. And they are, but only cursorily; you have a reputation for thoroughness and besides, it would be hard for your boss to think of a reason why you'd do such a thing for a random string of letters and numbers that could signify anybody, anybody at all, probably somebody you'd clash with if you met them. You never find out what happens to the people you assess, so you're all the more puzzled by what you're doing. Why can't you choose some other goal, a goal that at least includes the possibility of knowing whether you reached it or not? Face it; you're a bit of a weirdo. But whenever you feel you've gone too far with your tampering, you think of your grandmother and you press on.

Grandma is your dark inspiration. Your mother's mother made it out of a fallen communist state with an unseemly heap of valuables and a strangely blank-slate of a memory when it comes to recalling those hair-raising years. But she has such a sharp memory for so many other things – price changes, for instance. Your grandmother is vehement on the topic of survival and sceptical of all claims that it's possible to choose anything else when the chips are down. The official story is that it was Grandma's dentistry skills that kept her in funds. But her personality makes it seem more likely that she was a backstabber of monumental proportions. You take great pains to keep your suspicions from her, and she seems to get a kick out of that.

But how terrible you and your family are going to feel if, having thought of her as actively colluding with one of history's most murderous regimes, some proof emerges that Grandma was an ordinary dentist just like she said? A dentist subject to the kind of windfall that has been known to materialise for honest, well-regarded folk, in this case a scared but determined woman who held onto that windfall with both hands, scared and determined and just a dentist, truly. But she won't talk about any of it, that's the thing. *Cannot* you could all understand, or at least have sincere reverence for. But *will* not?

Your grandmother's Catholicism seems rooted in her approval of two saints whose reticence shines through the ages: St John of Nepomuk, who was famously executed for his insistence on keeping the secrets of the confessional, and St John Ogilvie, who went to his death after refusing to name those of his acquaintance who shared his faith. In lieu of a crucifix your grandmother wears a locket around her neck, and in that locket is a miniature reproduction of a painting featuring St John of Nepomuk, some tall-helmeted soldiers, a few horrified bystanders, four angels and a horse. In the painting the soldiers are pushing St J of N off the Charles Bridge, but St J of N isn't all that bothered, is looking up as if already hearing future confessions and interceding for his tormentors in advance. *Boys will be boys*, Father, St J of N's expression seems to say. The lone horse seems to agree. It's the sixteenth century, and the angels are there to carry St John of Nepomuk down to sleep on the river bed, where his halo of five stars awaits him. This is a scene your grandmother doesn't often reveal, but sometimes you see her fold a hand around the closed locket and it looks like she's toying with the idea of tearing it off the chain.

Suspect me if that's what you want to do.

What's the point of me saying any more than I've said... is it eloquence that makes you people believe things?

You are all morons.

These are the declarations your grandmother makes, and then you and your siblings all say: 'No, no, Grandma, what are you talking about, what do you mean, where did you get this idea?' without daring to so much as glance at each other.

You were in nursery school when your grandmother unexpectedly singled you out from your siblings and declared you her protégé. At first all that seemed to mean was that she paid for your education. That was good news for your parents, and for your siblings too, since there was more to go around. And your gratitude is real but so is your eternal obligation. Having paid for most of what's gone into your head during your formative years, there's a sense in which Grandma now owns you. She phones you when entertainment is required and you have to put on formal wear, take your fiddle over to her house and play peasant dances for her and her chess-club friends. When you displease her she takes it out on your mother, and the assumption within the family is that if at any point it becomes impossible for Grandma to live on her own, you'll be her live-in companion. (Was your education really that great?) So when you think of her, you think that you might as well do what you can while you can still do it.

Eva's popularity grows even as her speech becomes ever more monosyllabic. Susie, normally so focused on her work, spends a lot of time trying to get Eva to talk. Kathleen takes up shopping during her lunch break; she tries to keep her purchases concealed but occasionally you glimpse what she's stashing away in her locker – expensive-looking replicas of Eva's charity-shop chic. The interested singletons give Eva unprompted information about their private lives to see what she does with it, but she just chuckles and doesn't reciprocate. You want to ask her if she's sure she isn't a loner but you haven't spoken to her since she rejected your advice. Then Eva's office fortunes change. On a Monday morning Susie runs in breathless from having taken the stairs and says: 'Eva, there's someone here to see you! She's coming up in the lift and she's... crying?'

Another instance in which glass lift doors would be beneficial. Not to Eva, who already seems to know who the visitor is and looks around for somewhere to hide, but glass doors would have come in handy for everybody else in the office, since nobody knows what to do or say or think when the lift doors open to reveal a woman in tears and a boy of about five or so, not yet in tears but rapidly approaching them – there's that lip wobble, oh no. The woman looks quite a lot like Eva might look in a decade's time, maybe a decade and a half. As soon as this woman sees Eva, she starts saying things like, 'Please, please, I'm not even angry, I'm just saying please leave my husband alone, we're a family, can't you see?'

Eva backs away, knocking her handbag off her desk as she does so. Various items spill out but she doesn't have time to gather them up – the woman and child advance until they have her pinned up against the stationary-cupboard door. The woman falls to her knees and the boy stands beside her, his face scrunched up; he's crying so hard he can't see. 'You could so easily find someone else but I can't, not now... do you think this won't happen to you too one day? Please just stop seeing him, let him go...'

Eva waves her hands and speaks, but whatever excuse or explanation she's trying to make can't be heard above the begging. You say that someone should call security and people say they agree but nobody does anything. You're seeing a lot of folded arms and pursed lips. Kathleen mutters something about 'letting the woman have her say'. You call security yourself and the woman and child are led away. You pick Eva's things up from the floor and throw them into her bag. One item is notable: a leather-bound diary with a brass lock on it. A quiet woman with a locked book. Eva's beginning to intrigue you. She returns to her desk and continues working. Everybody else returns to their desks to send each other emails about Eva… at least that's what you presume is happening. You're not copied into any of those emails but everybody except you and Eva seems to be receiving a higher volume of messages than normal. You look at Eva from time to time and the whites of her eyes have turned pink but she doesn't look back at you or stop working. Fax, fax, photocopy. She answers a few phone calls and her tone is on the pleasant side of professional.

An anti-Eva movement emerges. Its members are no longer fooled by her glamour; Eva's a personification of all that's put on earth solely to break bonds, scrap commitments, prevent the course of true love from running smooth. You wouldn't call yourself pro-Eva, but bringing a small and distressed child to the office to confront your husband's mistress does strike you as more than a little manipulative. Maybe you're the only person who thinks so: that side of things certainly isn't discussed. Kathleen quickly distances herself from her attempts to imitate Eva. Those who still feel drawn to Eva become indignant when faced with her continued disinterest in making friends. Who does she think she is? Can't she see how nice they are?

'Yes, she should be grateful that people are still asking her out,' you say, and most of the people you say this to nod, pleased that you get where they're coming from, though Susie, Paul and a couple of the others eye you suspiciously. Susie takes to standing behind you while you're working sometimes, and given your clandestine meddling, this watchful presence puts you on edge. It's best not to mess with Susie.

One lunchtime, Eva brings her sandwich over to your desk and you eat together; this is sudden but after that you can no longer mock others by talking shit about Eva; she might overhear you and misunderstand. You ask Eva about her diary and she says she started writing it the year she turned thirteen. She'd just read *The Diary of Anne Frank* and was shaken by a voice like that falling silent, and then further shaken by the thought of all the voices who fell silent before we could ever have heard from them.

'And, you know – fuck everyone and everything that takes all these articulations of moodiness and tenderness and cleverness away. Not that I thought that's how I was,' Eva says. 'I was trying to figure out how to be a better friend, though, just like she was. I just thought I should keep a record of that time. Like she did. And I wrote it from thirteen to fifteen, like she did.'

You ask Eva if she felt like something was going to happen to her, too.

'Happen to me?'

You give her an example. 'I grew up in a city where people fell out of windows a lot,' you say. 'So I used to practice falling out of them myself. But after a few broken bones, I decided it's better just to not stand too close to windows.'

Eva gives you a piercing look. 'No, I didn't think anything was going to happen to me. It's all pretty ordinary teen stuff in there. Your city, though... is 'falling out of windows' a euphemism? And when you say 'fell', or even 'window', are you talking about something else?'

'No! What made you think that?'

'Your whole manner is really indirect. Sorry if that's rude.'

'It's not rude,' you say. You've already been told all about your indirectness, mostly by despairing ex-girlfriends.

'Can I ask one more question about the diary?'

Eva gives a cautious nod.

'Why do you still carry it around with you if you stopped writing in it years ago?'

'So I always know where it is,' she says.

Susie gets restless.

'Ask Miss Hoity-Toity if she's still seeing her married boyfriend,' she says to you.

You tell her you won't be doing that.

'The atmosphere in this office is so *stagnant*,'

Susie says, and decides to try and make Miss
Hoity-Toity resign. You don't see or hear anyone
openly agreeing to help Susie achieve this objective,
but then they wouldn't do that in your presence,
given that you now eat lunch with Eva every day.
So when Eva momentarily turns her back on
some food she's just bought and looks round to
find the salad knocked over so that her desk is
coated with dressing; when Eva's locker key is
stolen and she subsequently finds her locker full of
condoms; when Eva's sent a legitimate-looking file
attachment that crashes her computer for a few
hours and nobody else can spare the use of theirs
for even a minute, you just look straight at Susie
even though you know she isn't acting alone.
Susie's power trip has come so far along that she
goes around the office snickering with her eyes
half-closed. Is it the job that's doing this to you all?
Or do these games get played no matter what the
circumstances? A new girl has to be friendly and
morally upright; she should open up, just pick
someone and open up to them, make her choices
relatable. 'I didn't know he was married' would've
been well received, no matter how wooden the
delivery of those words. Just give us *something* to
start with, Miss Hoity-Toity.

Someone goes through Eva's bag and takes her
diary; when Eva discovers this she stands up at

her desk and asks for her diary back. She offers money for it: 'Whatever you want,' she says. 'I know you guys don't like me, and I don't like you either, but come on. That's two years of a life. Two years of a life.'

Everyone seems completely mystified by her words. Kathleen advises Eva to 'maybe check the toilets' and Eva runs off to do just that, comes back empty-handed and grimacing. She keeps working, and the next time she goes to the printer there's another print-out waiting for her on top of her document: RESIGN & GET THE DIARY BACK.

Eva demonstrates her seriousness regarding the diary by sub-mitting her letter of resignation the very same day. She says goodbye to you but you don't answer. In time she could have beaten Susie and co., could have forced them to accept that she was just there to work, but she let them win. Over what? Some book? Pathetic.

The next day, George 'finds' Eva's diary next to the coffee machine, and when you see his ungloved hands you notice what you failed to notice the day before – he and everybody except you and Eva wore gloves indoors all day. To avoid leaving fingerprints on the diary, you suppose. Nice; this can only mean that your co-workers have more issues than you do.

You volunteer to be the one to give Eva her

diary back. The only problem is you don't have her address, or her phone number – you never saw her outside work. HR can't release Eva's contact details; the woman isn't in the phonebook and has no online presence. You turn to the diary because you don't see any other option. You try to pick the lock yourself and fail, and your elder sister whispers: 'Try Grandma...'

'Oh, diary locks are easy,' your grandmother says reproachfully (what's the point of a protégée who can't pick an easy-peasy diary lock?). She has the book open in no time. She doesn't ask to read it; she doubts there's anything worthwhile in there. She tells you that the diary looks cheap; that what you thought was leather is actually imitation leather. Cheap or not, the diary has appeal for you. Squares of floral-print linen dot the front and back covers, and the pages are feather-light. The diarist wrote in violet ink.

Why I don't like to talk any more, you read, and then avert your eyes and turn to the page that touches the back cover. There's an address there, and there's a good chance this address is current, since it's written on a scrap of paper that's been taped over other scraps of paper with other addresses written on them. You copy the address down onto a different piece of paper and then stare, wondering how it can be that letters and numbers you've written with a black pen have come out violet-coloured. Also – also, while you were looking for pen and paper the diary has been unfolding. Not growing, exactly, but it's sitting upright on your tabletop and seems to fill or absorb the air around it so that the air turns this way and that, like pages. In fact, the book is like a hand and you, your living room and everything in it are pages being turned this way and that. You go towards the book, slowly and reluctantly – if only you could close this book remotely – but the closer you get to the book the greater the waning of the light in the room, and it becomes more difficult to actually move; in fact it is like walking through a paper tunnel that is folding you in, and there's chatter all about you: *Speak up, Eva*, and Eva, *you talk so fast, slow down* and *So you like to talk a lot, huh?* You hear: *You do know what you're saying, don't you?* and *Excuse me, missy, isn't there something you ought to be saying right now?* and *You just say that one more time!* You hear: *Shhh* and *So... do any of you guys know what she's talking about?* and *OK, but what's that got to do with anything?* and *Did you hear what she just said?*

It's mostly men you're hearing, or at least they sound male. But not all of them. Among the women Eva can be heard shushing herself. You chant and shout and cuckoo call. You recite verse, whatever's good, whatever comes to mind. This is how you pass through the building of Eva's quietness, and as you make that racket of yours you get close enough to the book to seize both covers (though you can no longer see them) and slam the book shut. Then you sit on it for a while, laughing hysterically, and after that you slide along the floor with the book beneath you until you find a roll of masking tape and wind it around the closed diary. Close shave, kiddo, close shave.

At the weekend you go to the address you found in the diary and a grey-haired, Levantine-looking man answers the door. Eva's lover? First he tells you Eva's out, then he says: 'Hang on, tell me again who you're looking for?'

You repeat Eva's name and he says that Eva doesn't actually live in that house. You ask since when, and he says she never lived there. But when you tell him you've got Eva's diary he lets you in: 'I think I saw her on the roof once.' His reluctance to commit to any statement of fact feels vaguely political. You go up onto the rooftop with no clear idea of whether Eva will be there or not. She's not. You look out over tiny gardens, big parking lots and satellite dishes. A glacial wind slices at the tops of your ears. If you were a character in a film this would be a good rooftop on which to battle and defeat some urban representative of the forces of darkness. You place the diary on the roof ledge and turn to go, but then you hear someone shout:

'Hey! Hey — is that mine?'

It's Eva. She's on the neighbouring rooftop. She must have emerged when you were taking in the view. The neighbouring rooftop has a swing set up on it, two seats side by side, and you watch as Eva launches herself out into the horizon with perfectly pointed toes, falls back, pushes forward again. She doesn't seem to remember you even though she only left a few days ago; this says as much about you as it does about her. You tell Eva that even though it looks as if her diary has been vigorously thumbed through, you're sure the contents remain secret. 'I didn't read it, anyway,' you say. The swing creaks as Eva sails up into the night sky, so high it almost seems as if she has no intention of coming back. But she does. And when she does, she says: 'So you still think that's why I locked it?'

About the Authors

Will Eaves was born in Bath in 1967 and educated at Beechen Cliff Comprehensive and King's College, Cambridge. He worked for twenty years as a journalist and was the Arts Editor of the *Times Literary Supplement* from 1995 to 2011. He teaches in the Writing Programme at the University of Warwick. He is the author of four novels: *The Oversight* (Picador, 2001; shortlisted for the Whitbread – now Costa – First Novel Award), *Nothing To Be Afraid Of* (Picador, 2005; shortlisted for the Encore Award), *This Is Paradise* (Picador, 2012), and *The Absent Therapist* (CB Editions, 2014; shortlisted for the Goldsmiths Prize); and two collections of poetry: *Sound Houses* (Carcanet, 2011) and *The Inevitable Gift Shop* (CB Editions, 2016; shortlisted for the Ted Hughes Award for New Work in Poetry). He lives in Brixton, London.

Jenni Fagan was born in Livingston, Scotland, and lives in Edinburgh. She has been nominated for the Pushcart Prize and was shortlisted for the Dundee International Book Prize, the Desmond

Elliott Prize, and the James Tait Black Prize for her debut novel *The Panoptican* (2012). In 2013, she was selected as one of Granta's Best Young British Young Novelists and appointed as a writer-in-residence at the University of Edinburgh. *The Sunlight Pilgrims* (2016) is her second novel.

Cynan Jones was born near Aberaeron on the west coast of Wales in 1975. He is the author of five novels, *The Long Dry, Everything I Found on the Beach, The Dig, Bird, Blood, Snow* and *Cove*.
His work is widely translated, and short stories have appeared on BBC Radio 4 and in a number of anthologies and publications including *Granta Magazine* and *The New Yorker*. He also scripted an episode of the television crime drama *Hinterland*.
He has won a Betty Trask Award, the Wales Book of the Year Fiction Prize, and a Jerwood Fiction Prize, and a chapter of *The Dig* was shortlisted for the Sunday Times EFG Private Bank Short Story Award in 2013. His latest novel *Cove* is currently longlisted for the Europese Literatuurprijs (in the Netherlands).

Benjamin Markovits grew up in Texas, London, Oxford and Berlin. He left an unpromising career as a professional basketball player to study the Romantics – an experience he wrote about in *Playing Days*, a novel. Since then he has taught high school English, worked at a left-wing cultural magazine, and written essays, stories and reviews for, among other publications, *The New York Times*, *Esquire*, *Granta*, *The Guardian*, *The London Review of Books* and *The Paris Review*. He has published seven novels, including *Either Side of Winter*, about a New York private school, and a trilogy on the life of Lord Byron: *Imposture*, *A Quiet Adjustment* and *Childish Loves*. His most recent novel, *You Don't Have To Live Like This*, about an experimental community in Detroit, won the James Tait Black Prize for Fiction in 2015. In 2009 he was a fellow of the Radcliffe Institute for Advanced Study at Harvard and won a Pushcart Prize for his short story *Another Sad, Bizarre Chapter in Human History*. Granta selected him as one of the Best of Young British Novelists in 2013. Markovits lives in London and is married, with a daughter and a son. He teaches Creative Writing at Royal Holloway, University of London.

Helen Oyeyemi is the author of several highly acclaimed novels, including *The Icarus Girl* (2005); *The Opposite House* (2007); *White is for Witching* (2009), which won a Somerset Maugham Award and was a Shirley Jackson Award finalist; *Mr Fox* (2011) and *Boy, Snow, Bird* (2014), which was a finalist for the *Los Angeles Times* Book Prize. Her short story collection, *What is not yours is not* *yours* was published in 2016 and won the PEN Open Book Award. Helen was selected as one of *Granta*'s Best Young British Novelists in 2013. She studied social and political sciences at Corpus Christi, Cambridge. She lives in Prague.

About the BBC National Short Story Award with BookTrust

The BBC National Short Story Award with BookTrust is one of the most prestigious for a single short story and celebrates the best in home-grown short fiction. The ambition of the Award, which is now in its twelfth year, is to expand opportunities for British writers, readers and publishers of the short story, and honour the UK's finest exponents of the form. James Lasdun secured the inaugural Award in 2006 for 'An Anxious Man'. In 2012 when the Award expanded internationally for one year, Miroslav Penkov was victorious for his story, 'East of the West'.

Last year, the Award was won by K J Orr for her story 'Disappearances'. Sarah Hall, Jonathan Buckley, Julian Gough, Clare Wigfall, Kate Clanchy and David Constantine have also carried off the Award with authors shortlisted in previous years including Zadie Smith, Jackie Kay, William Trevor, Rose Tremain, and Naomi Alderman. In 2015, the Award was extended to under 18s via the BBC Young

Writers' Award. For more information on the Awards, visit www.bbc.co.uk/nssa and www.bbc.co.uk/ywa or #BBCNSSA #shortstories on Twitter.

Award partners:

BBC Radio 4 is the world's biggest single commissioner of short stories, which attract more than a million listeners. Contemporary stories are broadcast every week, the majority of which are specially commissioned throughout the year. www.bbc.co.uk/radio4

BookTrust is the largest children's reading charity in Britain. We work to inspire a love of reading in children because we know that reading can transform lives. We give out over 3.5 million carefully chosen books to children throughout the UK; every parent receives a BookTrust book in the baby's first six months. Our books, guidance and resources are delivered via health, library, schools and early years practitioners, and are supported with advice and resources to encourage the reading habit. Reading for pleasure has a dramatic impact on educational outcomes, well-being and social mobility, and is also a huge pleasure in itself. We are committed to starting children on their reading journey and supporting them throughout. www.booktrust.org.uk